Brides of the DESERT ROSE

Harlequin American Romance
invites you to return to Bridle, Texas,
and the Desert Rose Ranch—
the scene of scandals and seduction
based on the bestselling **Texas Sheikhs** series....

In June discover how rivals become lovers.

IN THE ENEMY'S EMBRACE

by Mindy Neff
HAR #925

In July find out what happens
when a princess hides her identity.

AT THE RANCHER'S BIDDING

by Charlotte Maclay
HAR #929

In August celebrate the excitement
of a royal shotgun wedding.

BY THE SHEIKH'S COMMAND

by Debbi Rawlins
HAR #933

Don't miss any of these wonderful stories!

Dear Reader,

What better way to celebrate June, a month of courtship and romance, than with four new spectacular books from Harlequin American Romance?

First, the always wonderful Mindy Neff inaugurates Harlequin American Romance's new three-book continuity series, BRIDES OF THE DESERT ROSE, which is a follow-up to the bestselling TEXAS SHEIKHS series. *In the Enemy's Embrace* is a sexy rivals-become-lovers story you won't want to miss.

When a handsome aristocrat finds an abandoned newborn, he turns to a beautiful doctor to save the child's life. Will the adorable infant bond their hearts together and make them the perfect family? Find out in *A Baby for Lord Roderick* by Emily Dalton. Next, in *To Love an Older Man* by Debbi Rawlins, a dashing attorney vows to deny his attraction to the pregnant woman in need of his help. With love and affection, can the expectant beauty change the older man's mind? Sharon Swan launches her delightful continuing series WELCOME TO HARMONY with *Home-Grown Husband,* which features a single-mom gardener who looks to her mysterious and sexy new neighbor to spice up her life with some much-needed excitement and romance.

This month, and every month, come home to Harlequin American Romance—and enjoy!

Best,

Melissa Jeglinski
Associate Senior Editor
Harlequin American Romance

IN THE ENEMY'S EMBRACE

Mindy Neff

TORONTO • NEW YORK • LONDON
AMSTERDAM • PARIS • SYDNEY • HAMBURG
STOCKHOLM • ATHENS • TOKYO • MILAN • MADRID
PRAGUE • WARSAW • BUDAPEST • AUCKLAND

Special thanks and acknowledgment are given to Mindy Neff for her contribution to the BRIDES OF THE DESERT ROSE series.

ISBN 0-373-16925-6

IN THE ENEMY'S EMBRACE

This edition published by arrangement with Harlequin Books S.A.

Visit us at www.eHarlequin.com

Printed in U.S.A.

ABOUT THE AUTHOR

Mindy Neff published her first book with Harlequin American Romance in 1995. Since then, she has appeared regularly on the Waldenbooks bestseller list and won numerous awards, including the National Readers' Choice Award, the *Romantic Times* Career Achievement Award, as well as nominations for the prestigious RITA® Award.

Originally from Louisiana, Mindy settled in Southern California, where she married a really romantic guy and raised five great kids. Family, friends, writing and reading are her passions. When Mindy is not writing, her ideal getaway is a good book, hot sunshine and a chair at the river's edge at her second home in Parker, Arizona.

Mindy loves to hear from readers. You can write to her at P.O. Box 2704-262, Huntington Beach, CA 92647, or through her Web site at www.mindyneff.com, or e-mail at mindyneff@aol.com.

Books by Mindy Neff

HARLEQUIN AMERICAN ROMANCE

644—A FAMILY MAN
663—ADAM'S KISS
679—THE BAD BOY NEXT DOOR
711—THEY'RE THE ONE!*
739—A BACHELOR FOR THE BRIDE
759—THE COWBOY IS A DADDY
769—SUDDENLY A DADDY
795—THE VIRGIN & HER BODYGUARD*
800—THE PLAYBOY & THE MOMMY*
809—A PREGNANCY AND A PROPOSAL
830—THE RANCHER'S MAIL-ORDER BRIDE†
834—THE PLAYBOY'S OWN MISS PRIM†
838—THE HORSEMAN'S CONVENIENT WIFE†
857—THE SECRETARY GETS HER MAN
898—CHEYENNE'S LADY†
902—THE DOCTOR'S INSTANT FAMILY†
906—PREACHER'S IN-NAME-ONLY WIFE†
909—THE McCALLUM QUINTUPLETS
"Delivered with a Kiss"
925—IN THE ENEMY'S EMBRACE

*Tall, Dark & Irresistible
†Bachelors of Shotgun Ridge

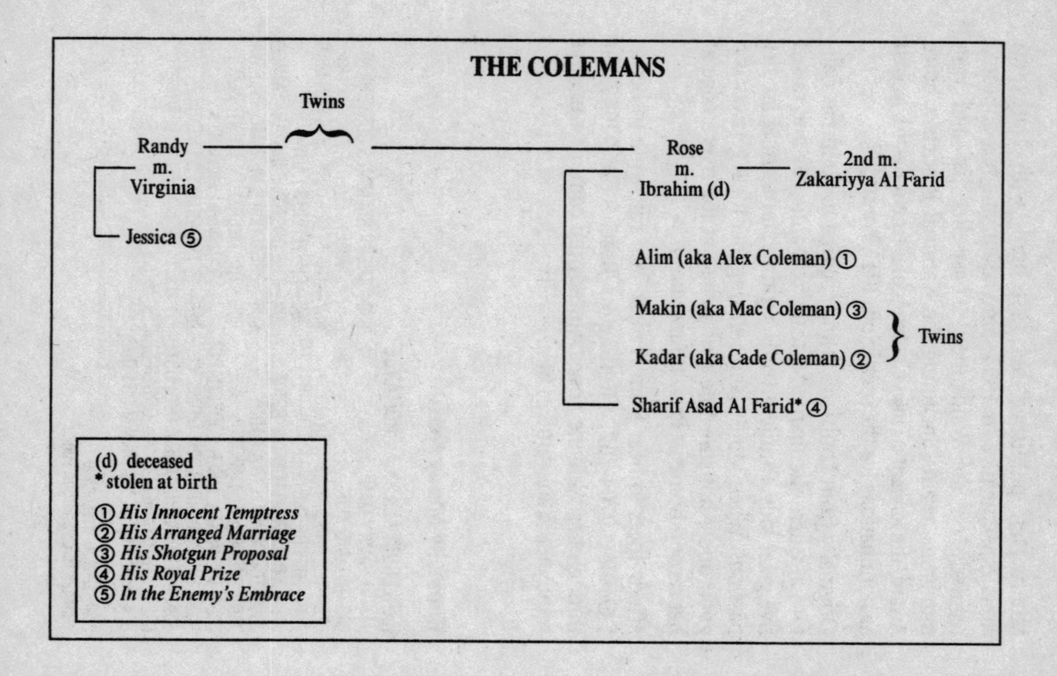
THE COLEMANS
Twins
Randy
m.
Virginia
Jessica ⑤
Rose
m.
Ibrahim (d)
2nd m.
Zakariyya Al Farid
Alim (aka Alex Coleman) ①
Makin (aka Mac Coleman) ③
Kadar (aka Cade Coleman) ②
Twins
Sharif Asad Al Farid* ④
(d) deceased
* stolen at birth
① His Innocent Temptress
② His Arranged Marriage
③ His Shotgun Proposal
④ His Royal Prize
⑤ In the Enemy's Embrace

Chapter One

Jessica Coleman hugged the scratchy wool blanket around her shoulders and shivered in the balmy June night air, the tremors from nerves, not cold.

Before her, the downtown Dallas apartment she'd called home for the past two months oozed smoke out its balcony windows like a baby dragon throwing a hissy fit.

Jessica felt a little like throwing a hissy fit herself, but realized it would do no good. Roll with the punches, her cousins always told her, stand proud and project a regal presence even if you don't feel it.

Easy for them to say. Her cousins, whom she'd been raised with, were indeed royalty. Bona fide sheikhs. All of them married now—thanks in part to Jessica's matchmaking skills.

She sniffed and wiped her nose on the scratchy blanket the firefighter had given her, her throat burning from the cloying smell of smoke. Destruction was always so painful to see. Especially destruction of a person's home.

Thankfully Jessica wasn't emotionally attached to the apartment, didn't have any keepsakes there—other than the photographs of her parents and cousins that she'd snatched up and shoved in her purse on her way out of the smoke-filled building. The rest of her belongings of any value to her were at home on the Desert Rose Ranch in Bridle, Texas, northwest of Austin.

Except her clothes of course. Now *that* was a big loss.

On the bright side, though, losing one's entire wardrobe was a great excuse to go shopping.

She glanced around at her neighbors and felt badly about her frivolous thought. My gosh, what was wrong with her? Was she on the verge of hysteria?

Unlike her, she imagined these people *had* lost irreplaceable keepsakes and memories. A couple had nearly lost their lives. That thought made her shiver—especially as the image of little Timmy, her neighbor's boy, sliding on his stomach toward an open flame replayed in her mind like a preview clip of a horror movie. He'd broken away from his parents, running back toward his apartment to search for his cat. The untied shoelaces on his sneakers had tripped him and sent him tumbling.

Tugging her mass of red hair from beneath the blanket, she turned at the sound of tires screeching on asphalt. Her heart lurched into her throat.

A black Mercedes sedan.

Nick Grayson—her absentee boss.

Well, sort of her boss. He was the son of the Grayson

half of Coleman-Grayson Investment Company, and she was the daughter of the Coleman half. His handsome features made her knees weak, yet his bossiness left her spitting like a she-cat more often than not. She knew her parents had asked him to watch over her, teach her the ropes in the family business, but at twenty-five, she was well past needing a baby-sitter and resented his superior attitude.

She sighed, watching him approach. His long stride and rigidly set shoulders beneath a black polo shirt didn't bode well for harmony. At least not between the two of them.

The subtle smell of sandalwood cologne surrounded her as he drew near, giving her a second's respite from the acrid stench of smoke. Heat coursed through her. Her insides still trembled like soft-set pudding—nerves and something more now.

Why in the world couldn't she be her normal "catch me if you can, baby" self around this man? It was thoroughly disquieting, a failing she'd had since she was thirteen. You'd think she would've gotten over her adolescent crush.

"Are you all right?" he asked, his deep voice concerned, edgy.

Annoyed that she wanted to say no and turn into his wide chest for comfort, Jessica clutched the blanket more snugly around her shoulders. "Do you have spies? Had my phones tapped? What?" Why was it he always showed up when she needed him?

She didn't *want* to need him, even though the smell

of his skin and the intensity of his dark-brown eyes made her heart do cartwheels in her chest.

"Did you make a phone call?" he asked, his tone dripping with censure. "I don't recall mine ringing."

When he cocked a dark brow in that sexy, annoying way of his, she didn't know whether to hit him or jump his bones.

"Obviously it must have rung sometime," she said. "Otherwise, why would you show up like a thief with a posse on his tail?"

"A thief?"

She shrugged. "Black car, windows tinted black, dressed in all black. A person would think you're a bad guy or something."

The long look he gave her did indeed telegraph danger. Sexual, rather than physical.

"The color of the car isn't readily changeable. The clothes were what I put my hands on first in the closet. I was understandably anxious to get out of the house."

"You had ESP or something that drew you out of bed and told you my apartment building was burning down?"

"No. Guy Pirrazzo—he's the head of personnel at the company—"

"I know who Guy is," she said. She'd found that out on her own. She'd come to Coleman-Grayson at her parents' behest to learn the ins and outs of the business under Nick Grayson's tutelage. He hadn't done much tutoring so far. It was as though he was avoiding her, finding excuses to be out of the office or out of town altogether.

Although he *did* have an uncanny knack for showing up every time she seemed to be at her worst.

"Yes, well, Guy's uncle lives in this building—"

"Lived," she corrected waving a hand at the water-and-soot-drenched grounds. She didn't think she'd ever get the shrill scream of the smoke alarm out of her head. Emergency lights from the fire engines cast intermittent splashes of crimson across the wet asphalt, which had already been cordoned off with yellow tape.

"Lived," Nick repeated, his jaw flexing as though he was annoyed and holding on by a thread at being interrupted. "Guy recalled that you were in the same building and phoned to let me know about the fire."

He was looking at her as though he was disappointed that she hadn't called him herself, as though he'd expected as much.

Which was absurd of course. The man avoided her the way an Arabian horse shies around a Texas rattler.

At the moment, though, his demeanor was far from shy. It set her nerves tingling.

She cleared her throat, unsure what to say or do next. Suddenly she felt nervous and vulnerable. The adrenaline that had carried her out of the apartment building was ebbing. Despite the fact that Nick Grayson got on her nerves, a part of her was actually glad he was here.

She shoved her tousled red hair off her forehead and sighed.

Nick laid a gentle hand on her shoulder. "Are you ready to go?"

His quiet voice and warm breath sent more shivers down her spine. At this rate, her bones were likely to rattle apart joint by joint. "Go where?"

"My place, I'm thinking."

She looked up at him. "Obviously you're *not* thinking to make a suggestion like that."

Astonished, she watched his teeth flash white as his lips canted into a slow grin.

"Now, Jess. Are you insinuating the two of us can't get along under the same roof?"

"I'm not insinuating. I *know*."

He slung an arm around her shoulders, steered her toward his car. "Come on. Let's get out of here and we'll fight about it later."

She had to bite her lip to keep from smiling. If there was one thing she and Nick were good at, it was fighting. Well, sparring was probably more accurate.

He held the car door open for her and gallantly helped her into the plush leather seat as though she'd been harmed, not just her apartment.

"You could drop me at the Embassy Suites or the Sheraton."

"Sit back and relax. From the looks of that garage, I'd guess your car's pretty well toast. Since I'm in the driver's seat, I say we go to Grayson suites."

The sight of her ruined building sent another sickening tremor through her. "Since when are you in the hotel business?"

He slanted her a look. "Play on words, Red. I've got plenty of suites in my place. You'll be more comfortable there than at a hotel."

Jessica wasn't so sure about that. The words *comfortable* and *Nick Grayson* didn't coexist peacefully in her vocabulary. Right now, though, she was too tired to put up much of a fuss.

It was an effort to act tough, but she couldn't afford to let down her guard. Not with Nick.

She rested her head against the leather seat. Soft country music played on the stereo system. The lights on the dashboard looked sophisticated and complicated, yet pretty against the dark night. She shut her eyes as they wound through downtown Dallas, then left the city lights far behind as they traveled down a four-lane highway divided by a grassy median strip.

She heard the rustle of denim and cotton sliding against leather, knew he'd turned to look at her. She kept her eyes lowered. There was a time when she would have given her prize Arabian mare to be sitting next to Nick Grayson in his car, to have him be the dashing knight who'd come rushing to her rescue.

That seemed like a lifetime ago. She'd been a girl of thirteen and he'd been a worldly man of twenty-one. Even now, her face heated when she thought of that embarrassing day he'd come out to the Desert Rose Ranch. She'd been filled with a young girl's dreams, infatuated with this older boy, watched him, pined for him, ached for him to notice her as only a young girl in her first crush can ache.

He'd been sweet to her, and that was all it had taken for her to tumble head over heels. She'd been so sure of herself, feeling older now that she was a teen, certain that Nick Grayson would fall madly in lust with her, promise her undying love, promise to wait for her forever. She'd built up the scenario, dreamed it so often it had become real to her.

That had made his abrupt rejection all the more humiliating.

Feeling the familiar shame flutter in her stomach at the memory, she banished the thought and sat up straighter, looking around as he drove through a set of private gates supported by brick pillars. White wood fences glowed in the moonlight, reminding her of home, of the paddocks that held million-dollar Arabian champions. Where the Desert Rose was built in a Spanish architectural style, Nick's house was a scaled-down version of Southfork—the estate made famous by the long-running TV series *Dallas*.

"I guess our daddies pay you pretty well," she mused aloud.

He shot her a frowning look. "I work hard for the salary the company pays me."

Hmmm. She'd hit a nerve. She could practically hear his thoughts, the words he was civilized enough not to tack on. *I work hard for the salary the company pays me...unlike you.*

Perhaps his touchiness had something to do with the fact that the Coleman half of the partnership owned fifty-one percent of the voting stock, leaving the Graysons a mere forty-nine. Technically she had more clout than he did, but she decided not to poke at that particular sore tonight. She wasn't at her best. And to keep one step ahead of Nick Grayson, she *needed* to be at her best.

He stopped the car in the circular driveway beneath a porte-cochere and shut off the engine. A warm breeze lifted her hair as she got out of the car. Cicadas and crickets harmonized with the deeper hum of tree frogs, the sound pressing in on her ears.

She shivered. She'd grown up on a ranch, dealt with snakes and all manner of varmints, yet the thought of thousands of huge insects and critters blending in with the trees, watching her with their buggy eyes, gave her the creeps.

"You cold?" Nick asked as he reached past her to open the front door.

"No. It's those stupid locusts. I think they deliberately antagonize me because they can sense I don't like them."

A corner of his mouth kicked up. "I don't think you can go anywhere in Texas and get away from them."

"No place that has trees, that's for sure." She ducked under his outstretched arm and crossed the threshold to the foyer. A fortune in marble paved the floor, flowing like polished glass until it met the thick carpet of an enormous living room.

Jessica was impressed despite herself. Heck, she came from a wealthy family. But the layout of Nick's home was breathtaking.

A solid wall of windows beckoned her farther into the room, where comfortable leather furniture cohabited nicely with priceless antiques. Doors opened onto a patio, where subtle lighting turned the swimming pool into a fantasy-like paradise.

Unable to resist, she walked right out the doors, drawn by the water, and inhaled the scent of chlorine and the sweet perfume of honeysuckle vines.

He switched on the patio and yard lights, and Jessica was further awed. Manicured lawns, shaded by mature oak and elm trees, sloped down to a tranquil lake where a wooden dock extended out into the water. A sporty powerboat was moored at one side of the dock, tied to cleats and protected by bright orange buoys.

She turned to Nick, raised a brow. "A swimming pool *and* a lake?"

Hands in his pockets, he stood several feet away as though he didn't trust himself to come any closer. "I swim in the pool and fish in the lake."

"Ah, a man who knows how to bring home dinner."

He was silent, watching her as though she were a bobcat ready to pounce. She clearly made him nervous, and Jessica found this a delicious turn of events. She was no longer the thirteen-year-old girl with a mad crush, the girl who'd been humiliated when her kiss had been rebuffed. With her now twenty-five, the eight-year age difference put them in a completely different playing field.

And judging by the hungry look in his eyes, she had the home advantage.

"We should probably go in before the mosquitoes start biting," he said, his hands still in his pockets, his dark gaze trained on her.

"Vitamin B. I take it religiously and they never munch on me." Because it was past midnight and they were both a little punchy from the drama of the evening, she preceded him into the house and caught a glimpse of her reflection in the darkened windows when he turned off the outside lights.

For pity's sake. In all the hoopla, she'd completely forgotten that she still wore her Victoria's Secret pajamas. Oh, they were modest enough, thin sweatpants in a pink-and-red heart pattern and a matching tank top. Looking down, she noticed the insoles of her sandals were imprinted with toe-shaped smudges from the water and soot remnants of the fire.

She yelped and jumped up onto the fireplace hearth.

Nick took an immediate step forward, switching on the overhead lights, his gaze scanning the floor. "What?" He nearly shouted the word.

She knew he was imagining they'd let a critter in through the open doors, and she bit the inside of her cheek to keep from laughing. At this point, a bout of laughter might well turn into that hysteria she'd been worrying about earlier. "My feet are dirty."

"Your..."

She held up a foot, letting her white sandal dangle from her toes. Even her gold toe ring was tarnished black. "I hope I didn't track this mess on your beautiful carpet."

''The rugs can be cleaned, Red. My heart's not so easily repaired.''

''Sorry. I didn't mean to shake you up. And why do you keep scowling at me like that?''

''I'm not scowling.''

She rolled her eyes. ''Look in the mirror, why don't you. And while you're at it, could you bring me a towel so I can rake some of this gunk off my feet? Honestly, I should have jumped in the pool while I was out there.''

''I can give you a hand if you like.''

She looked at him and laughed. ''A push, you mean?''

A dimple creased his cheek. Amazing, since his expression was still nearly as solemn as a judge's.

He turned to leave the room, presumably to do her bidding. Man, oh, man, Nick Grayson had one fine derriere. Jessica sat down on the brick hearth and rested her chin on her raised knees, sniffed, then lifted her head. No wonder Nick was keeping a respectable distance between them. She reeked of smoke.

Her gaze was still on the seat of his jeans when he suddenly turned and caught her staring. Except now she was staring at the *fly* of his jeans.

She lifted her eyes to his scowling face. ''Well,'' she said. ''*You're* the one who turned around. If you'd just kept going, I could have ogled your backside in peace and you'd have been none the wiser....'' Her words dried up as he crossed the room toward her, bent down and scooped her up in his arms. "What in the world are you doing?"

"Taking you to the shower."

"Fetching a towel was too taxing for you?"

"My towels are white. You'd ruin them."

"The man owns a swimming pool *and* a lake and he quibbles over a towel." She sighed and clutched the blanket that was still around her shoulders.

"Red?"

"Mmm?"

"You smell like charred wood."

Yes, and if she closed her eyes, her mind replayed the horrible image of flames licking at her neighbor's window. "You're such a gentleman for pointing that out, Grayson. No sense complaining, though. I didn't ask for the impromptu ride."

"A good host should bear up under any hardship."

"Now I'm a hardship. You're not exactly endearing yourself to me."

"I wasn't trying to." He lowered her feet to the tile floor of the bathroom.

Jessica wasn't sure what imp got into her, but she dropped the blanket from her shoulders and turned to face him.

In a typically male reaction, his gaze dipped to her tank top where thin cotton adorned with little hearts stretched over her breasts. She felt her nipples harden and nearly groaned.

But she'd started this, and she wouldn't act like a shy maiden now. Never mind that she had little hands-on experience in the male-female relationship department; she'd learned years ago that men were drawn to the voluptuous curves of her body, and she'd perfected a seductress act that could have a guy panting like a puppy in two seconds flat. And while Nick wasn't exactly panting, his dark eyes flared nearly black—a perfect match for his clothes.

A muscle worked in his jaw as he backed out of the bathroom. "You didn't happen to stuff an extra change of clothes in that backpack purse, did you?"

"'Fraid not."

"I'll see what I can come up with."

He closed the door behind him and Jessica let out a slow breath. Her hands were trembling—heck, her entire insides were quaking.

Darn it, she was *not* attracted to Nick Grayson. She'd gotten over that years ago. They rubbed each other the wrong way, couldn't have a decent conversation without tempers igniting. So why the devil were her nipples poking out as if she'd just dipped herself in an icy lake?

Undressing, she turned on the shower, adjusted the water temperature and stuck her head under the steamy spray. From the corner of her eye, she saw the bathroom door open and she froze.

Holding her breath, she watched as a masculine arm reached in and set down a stack of folded clothes, then withdrew, pulling the door closed again. She let out a sigh, her heart pumping. She'd been raised in a house with three male cousins, but none of them had ever breached her privacy this way. Well, it hadn't actually been breached. He hadn't come all the way in the room and looked.

Just to ease her mind, she would make a point of standing at the doorway when she was done to see if the mirror afforded a clear view to the shower. No sense letting Nick Grayson get one up on her.

The purpose, she'd decided weeks ago, was to make *him* drool, regret what he'd so carelessly turned down years ago. *Not* the other way around.

NICK WENT INTO the kitchen and poured himself a healthy shot of brandy. He'd tried to work on a prospectus report for a software company he was considering investing in, but the sound of water rushing through the pipes was too much of a distraction. Especially knowing Jessica Coleman was the one standing naked in his shower.

Damn it, he should have just left the clothes outside the door. He'd only meant to stick his arm in and put the stuff on the counter. How the hell was he to know the mirror angle gave a perfect reflection of the shower—and its occupant? Now, in addition to a twelve-year-old kiss haunting him, he had the image of her naked curvy body to keep him up nights.

She could have been burned tonight, lost her life. That one vulnerable look she'd given him when he'd first shown up at the fire would forever be etched in his mind. It had said, *Hold me, please.* And he'd wanted to, wanted to take care of her, but he was scared to touch her.

Jessica Coleman had been off-limits for so long. He was weak when it came to her, didn't trust himself to let go, and that made him mad.

The very worst thing he could do was get involved with a Coleman. He and Jess had been like water and oil since the moment they'd met—flammable, volatile, *passionate* oil. Love and hate walked a very thin line. To act on that emotion, see where it would take them, was too dangerous. One or both of them would likely get burned. And what happened between them would naturally affect the business.

Coleman-Grayson Investment Company was too important to him to take a chance on ripping it apart because of personal conflict.

"Didn't your mama ever tell you what a shame it'd be if your face ended up getting stuck in that position?"

He looked up, became aware that his brows were indeed drawn together in a frown, then promptly lost his entire train of thought.

She wore a white bathrobe he kept for guests who came to swim. He could see the collar of his T-shirt he'd lent her beneath the plunging V of the robe. Her legs and feet were bare and he wondered if she was wearing the drawstring shorts he'd laid out for her. Her long red hair was a mass of damp curls, framing her face and sliding over her shoulders. Her face was void of makeup, making her look even younger. That should have had the effect of ice water dumped over his head, but it didn't.

Although she was perfectly decent, his body was humming as if she'd walked into the room stark naked.

Nerves crowded when she sauntered over to him, reached out and brushed his forehead with her finger.

"It's your skin, but seems a shame to promote early wrinkles like this." She plucked the brandy glass out of his hand, sipped, her gaze still on his.

Her eyes were unique, one green and the other blue—something he'd never seen on anyone before. That was the kind of thing that sticks in a man's mind. It'd stuck in his since the day he first laid eyes on her.

"Did you want a glass?" he asked.

"This one's fine. Why don't you just pour yourself another?"

Not many people came into his home and told him what to do. They wouldn't dare. Obviously Jessica Coleman dared.

He might have called a halt to it, but the sultry pitch of her voice, the seduction in those unique eyes, was rendering him stupid.

Determined to break the spell, he got down another crystal glass and poured brandy in it, putting distance between them in the process.

"Did you want me to show you to your room?"

She grinned. "Are you trying to tell me it's past my bedtime?"

"Do you have to challenge everything I say?"

"Habit, I suppose."

"Well, suppose you can break it?"

"A truce works two ways, you know."

He wasn't sure how a man could be annoyed and want to smile at the same time. Jessica Coleman just flat out confounded him.

"I'm game if you are," he said.

"Are you sure you don't want to give me a lift to the nearest hotel? I mean, practically tripping over each other like this will likely cramp both our styles."

"It's a big place. I doubt we'll trip."

"We'll definitely be aware of each other, though. And I, at least, have a fairly active social life."

"And what makes you think I don't?"

She shrugged. "I guess it's just hard to imagine. You're stuffy, all business. You never knew how to enjoy what was offered."

He saw the quickly masked distress in her eyes, knew she hadn't meant to blurt those words, knew that she was referring to that long-ago kiss. He knew he'd hurt her, but until now, hadn't realized the depth of that pain.

But damn it, she'd been jailbait back then, and he'd hated the pull of attraction he felt for the kid, fought it like crazy. All it had taken was a long look into those intriguing eyes filled with curiosity and mystery—yes, even at that young age, Jessica Coleman had exuded an innocent sensuality that promised bliss. She'd scared the hell out of him. And because of that, he'd mishandled her tender feelings, crushed her spirit.

But she was no longer a girl of thirteen, and the man in him had been goaded just about enough.

Obviously her crushed spirit had only been a temporary setback.

Chapter Two

Jessica's heart pounded as Nick deliberately stepped toward her, his dark eyes filled with intent. He crowded her, trapped her between his body and the kitchen cabinets, twined a finger around one of her damp curls and toyed with the end where it just brushed the slope of her breast, all the while holding her gaze with his.

"Careful how you taunt, cowgirl. We're all grown-up now."

Dear heaven, she hadn't realized how difficult it would be to keep up this act. She could well be out-matched, but she was darned if she'd give it up now.

"So nice of you to notice," she said, and neatly ducked beneath his arms. "Too bad I'm no longer interested."

"Is that a dare?"

Jessica tucked her hair behind her ear, fought to get the jolt of awareness under control. She knew she was playing with fire and needed to backtrack in a hurry. Nick Grayson was a worthy opponent, not someone to underestimate. "Of course not."

"Sounded that way to me. A statement of disinterest is practically an open invitation to prove just the opposite."

"Oh, for Pete's sake. Chill out, would you?" Actually, she was the one who needed to chill out. The man oozed seduction and danger from every masculine pore. She was fast finding herself in over her head. And that was not a position she wanted to be in.

She held up her hands to form a T. "Truce, okay? We've known each other for years. There's no reason in the world why we can't get along just fine as temporary roommates. I'll contact the insurance people in the morning and see if the contents of the apartment were covered."

"Since Coleman-Grayson owns the building, I don't imagine you'll have any trouble settling."

"Fine, then. As soon as I can find a new apartment and new furniture and stuff, I'll be out of your hair. Until then..." She moved forward and held out her hand. "Friends?"

He enveloped her hand in both of his. His palms were wide and warm, and she felt the oddest vibration shimmy up her arm.

"Friends," he agreed. "As for the house rules, make yourself at home—though I expect you to respect my privacy and go easy on the loud music and wild parties."

"Likewise." Why wasn't he letting go of her hand? And why was he staring into her eyes like that? The word that came to mind was *hungry*. She licked her lips. ''If you have a date or want to bring a lady home, I'll make myself scarce. Just warn me in advance.''

He took a step closer. ''So, I'm not too stuffy to date and have women friends?'' His voice was soft and deep and filled with a sensuality she didn't quite know how to respond to.

What was going on here? Sparks were literally zinging between them. Oh, she'd wanted to make Nick Grayson drool. But she hadn't counted on this sneak attack he seemed to be waging, setting *her* off balance.

Instead of answering his question, she said, ''Look...uh, I think we're both tired. I don't know about you, but being rudely wakened to find your house on fire is enough to...'' Her voice hitched and she cleared it. ''Enough to...'' Oh, Lord, she was going to cry. She could feel it and she was mortified. Her nose and throat burned, and her eyes stung.

She tried to back away, but Nick used their joined hands to pull her right into the comforting width of his chest.

''I wondered when that was going to catch up with you,'' he murmured, stroking her hair, her back, soothing her with the sweep of his wide palm. ''Shh, you're safe with me now, kiddo.''

Jessica stiffened. *Kiddo.* She didn't want him thinking about her as a kid, but obviously he did.

She stepped back. ''I'm fine. Really. I think I'll just turn in.''

The frown was back on his face. She watched his chest rise and fall with a deep breath, tried not to notice how his black polo shirt clung to the breadth of his physique.

She should have learned her lesson twelve years ago. Nick saw her merely as the daughter of a business partner. *She* was the one who kept getting mixed up, reading more into a look or touch than was actually there. It wasn't his fault that he was born with the kind of looks that naturally made a woman fantasize, forget who, what and where she was.

But Jessica *needed* to remember.

In his eyes, they would never be on an equal footing. She'd be the kid and he'd be the guy her parents had asked to watch over her.

And that simply wasn't acceptable.

He nodded and turned away from her. "I'll show you to your room."

FOR THE FIRST TIME in years, Nick overslept. Shrugging into his suit jacket, he finished knotting his tie as he went down the stairs. He was debating whether to head on out the front door and grab coffee at the office, or take the time to drink it here when he heard voices and laughter coming from the kitchen.

Jessica's sultry, unrestrained laughter, and the deeper, carefree chortle of his younger brother, Chase.

He'd forgotten that Chase was due home for his annual visit. At twenty-five, his brother had yet to settle on what he wanted to be when he grew up. At present, he fancied himself a carefree playboy, with Europe as his playground of choice.

Well, that wasn't exactly so, or fair. Chase raced cars and yachts and made a fortune at it. He was the kind of guy who'd wither away if he had to sit behind a desk or preside over meetings all day.

Jealousy speared Nick right in the solar plexus when he stopped in the kitchen doorway. It was a new emotion and it bothered him.

Jessica, still wearing the clothes Nick had given her last night—minus the robe, he noted—was sitting at the kitchen table chatting with Chase. They were both the same age, so easily enjoyed a good laugh. Just watching them made Nick feel sixty-three, instead of thirty-three.

For as long as he could remember, he'd been the responsible one, the sensible one, the driven one. Had he ever let himself laugh the way Chase was doing now?

And what the hell was so funny, anyway? He didn't like this feeling of being on the outside.

"You're up and about early this morning," he said.

Chase looked up and grinned. "And you're late, big brother." Chase stood and enveloped Nick in a hug. "Good to see you slacking off a bit. And with such beautiful company."

"She's not company."

"Oh? Sorry, I didn't know you were living with somebody."

"I'm not—"

"Oh, stop teasing him, Chase," Jessica said. "He's

pulling your chain, Nick. I already told him about the fire."

Nick moved over to the coffeepot and poured himself a cup. He needed a shot of caffeine to clear his head.

"It made the paper," Chase said. "Our Jess is a heroine. Saved a kid and his cat."

"The media exaggerates." Jessica scooted the newspaper aside. She'd done what needed to be done, didn't want the accolades the paper had given her, didn't want to think about what *might* have happened if she hadn't seen Timmy Matheson trip and fall. The fearlessness of children, she thought. While everyone else had been scrambling for an exit, Timmy had ignored his mother's screams and charged back toward their burning apartment.

"Did the papers say how the fire started?" Nick asked.

"Paint cans too close to a water heater."

"That'll do it. You'll want to call your folks. Chances are the story made the Bridle paper, as well."

"I already called." She resisted the urge to tack on *sir.* "And I called the office this morning, too. Steve's going to get the ball rolling with the insurance company and check on the painting contractor's coverage, as well." Steve Tyler worked in accounting at Coleman-Grayson.

"Busy girl."

"I usually am." Not that he would know that firsthand, given the way he'd been avoiding the office lately. Ever since she'd come to work there. "By the way, I'm taking the day off to shop for a replacement wardrobe. I've already called Rhonda to let her know I won't be in."

"If I didn't have a prior commitment," Chase said, "I'd offer to go with you and carry your packages."

"A man who actually likes to shop? Be still my heart." She glanced at Nick. "Are you sure the two of you are brothers? Mr. All Business Nick probably wouldn't think of taking time off to carry a woman's shopping bags."

"On the contrary," Nick said, leaning back against the counter, "I'd enjoy a day at the mall."

Caught off guard, Jessica's jaw dropped.

Amusement and satisfaction danced in his eyes. "A good business lesson, Red. Never make a firm statement that you can't back up with fact. How does nine-forty-five suit you?"

She regained her composure. "It suits me, um, fine—provided I can find something decent to wear in public." She'd thrown away her smoke-drenched pajamas, and the only thing she had left was what she was wearing—the drawstring shorts and T-shirt Nick had lent her to sleep in.

"You look pretty decent to me," Chase commented with a waggle of his eyebrows.

"Don't you have someplace you need to be?" Nick asked him.

Chase grinned. "Yeah. I guess I should go check in

with the folks, let them know I'm in town. I imagine they'll want to get us all together for dinner.''

Nick nodded. ''Just let me know when.''

''Will do.'' Chase lifted Jessica's hand and gallantly bowed over it, placing a kiss on her knuckles. ''It was great to see you again, Jess. *Really* great. I'll call you.''

''I'll hold you to it,'' she said.

Nick had trouble swallowing his coffee and was barely civilized enough to shake Chase's hand as his brother left.

What was Chase thinking? Had he forgotten that they'd both made a pact not to date friends of the family? Three years ago Chase had been engaged to the daughter of their mother's best friend. Everything had been fine until the relationship shattered. Ugly words and accusations had flown from both sides. There were squabbles over money, the diamond engagement ring and who was at fault. Both families had been dragged into the fray, each forced to choose sides, effectively ruining a long-standing friendship.

When it came to Jessica, not only did they risk ruining another friendship, but a business partnership, as well.

''There's that charming expression I've come to know and love,'' Jessica said as she got up from the table and walked toward him. She brushed a finger over his forehead, and he jerked back so fast he nearly spilled his coffee.

She grinned. ''Got any girl clothes around here?''

''None that come to mind. If you want, you can rummage through my closet and see if anything will fit. I've got workout clothes you can probably make do with."

"See how well we're doing with our truce? I'm sleeping in your bed and wearing your clothes—all in the space of a day. Pretty darn good if you ask me."

Nick choked on a swallow of hot coffee. Jessica helpfully thumped him on the back and sashayed out of the room.

God almighty, he wasn't sure he'd survive that woman.

THE GALLERIA MALL in Dallas was a shopper's paradise. And Nick soon found out that Jessica was an expert at the sport of shopping and could cull choice merchandise off every sale rack like a pro.

He'd discarded his suit jacket an hour ago outside the dressing room of Macy's. Now, slouched in a chair outside yet another dressing room—Nordstrom's this time—he loosened the knot of his tie and punched in another number on his cell phone. The reception inside the store was the pits, and after being cut off for the third time, he switched it off.

He'd made a huge mistake by letting Jessica goad him. His pride had gotten in the way and look where he was. She kept sauntering out of the dressing rooms, wearing outfit after outfit, asking his opinion as though they were girlfriends instead of business partners. A bag sat at his feet filled with lingerie she *hadn't* modeled for him—thank God. The images his mind was supplying made him sweat.

Toeing the bag a little farther away so it would quit antagonizing him, he looked up and nearly dropped the phone in his hand and his senses to boot.

She wore a siren-red dress that clung to every sweet curve of her body and made him think of hot sex and endless nights.

"Well?" she asked, and executed a pirouette.

He cleared his throat. "Not exactly office attire."

She glanced at him over her shoulder. His heart slammed against his chest. He wondered if she'd done it on purpose, if she knew how sexy that pose was, the way her raised arms pulled the material over her breasts as she lifted her hair off her neck, piling it on top of her head.

"Too much, hmm?"

"I didn't say that."

She turned to face him. "Then what *do* you say?"

"It's very…nice." *Total understatement.* He'd gone from zip to hard in two seconds flat. No way could he stand up at the moment without embarrassing himself. And damned if he'd give her the satisfaction of knowing she'd gotten to him. The imp was having too much fun as it was. If he wasn't mistaken, she was deliberately being seductive.

"I probably shouldn't get it. I don't know where I'd wear it."

"What about that hot and heavy social life you were talking about?"

She gave him a smile that nearly knocked the breath out of him. Not the put-on smile of a seductress. A sweet smile. An easy smile. "To tell the truth, my social life's not as hot and heavy as I might have led you to believe."

Just that simply, with that easy honesty, Nick felt his guard drop. About the time he thought he had her figured out, she did an about-face and said something that blew his perception of her out of the water.

Despite his best intentions to keep his distance and his control around Jessica Coleman, her innate charm was too much to resist.

"That dress was made for you, Red. You should get it."

She gave him a grin. "Okay. That's about all the arm twisting I need to...yikes!"

"What?"

"Did you see the price tag on this thing?" She flashed it in front of his face, then shook her head and whirled around. "Forget it."

Dumbfounded, Nick watched her disappear back into the dressing room. The woman was a mass of contradictions. She could afford to buy ten dresses and pay double what the price tag said. The fact that she wouldn't intrigued him. He'd always thought Jessica Coleman was pampered and spoiled, with nothing more pressing on her mind than shopping and parties. Lately he'd had to rethink quite a few of his preconceived notions.

And how many of those notions were his own defense mechanisms kicking in? Was he intent on finding fault in hopes of diluting the sexual sizzle he felt every time she walked into a room?

He didn't know the answers. He did know, however, that the "come and get me, baby" red dress had her name written on it.

After summoning the salesclerk, he said, "The red dress the young lady was just trying on? Put it on my charge, gift wrap it and mail it to this address." He handed her a business card, along with his credit card.

"A surprise?" the clerk asked.

"Yes."

"I'll be the soul of discretion."

"YOU KNOW, I usually prefer to shop alone," Jessica said, glancing up at the Galleria's dramatic glass atrium above them. "And frankly, I was dreading you tagging along today. I couldn't believe you actually volunteered."

"I only did because you were so sure I wouldn't."

She bumped her shoulder against his. The silky material of the summery dress she'd bought at the first department store felt good against her skin, made her feel like herself again. A trip to the makeup counter and a complimentary makeover had her skin glowing and her eyes and mouth enhanced to where she felt the score between them was a bit more even. It had been torture walking into a mall with a gorgeous man when she was wearing oversize clothing and her face was naked.

''Well, now you're in it for the duration.''

''You mean you're not done?'' He looked toward one of the exit doors on the mall's lower level. Sunlight pierced the glass ceiling overhead, splashing rainbows over the gleaming floors.

''I need shoes, Grayson. Lots of them. Where is your shopping spirit?''

''I think I lost it back between the Levi's and Guess jeans.''

''I don't know why you wouldn't tell me which pair looked better on my butt.''

''Don't start, Red. I do have a healthy amount of self-preservation.''

''Well, see if I ever take you shopping with me again,'' she huffed dramatically.

''Please don't.''

She laughed and bumped his shoulder again. ''You're being a pretty good sport. I'm surprised.''

''There's probably a lot about me that would surprise you.''

''Give it a try. Tell me something about you—schooldays, let's say.''

''What, like a truth-or-dare kind of thing?''

''Hmm, that could get interesting.'' Though not what she'd had in mind. ''I'm game if you are.''

He shook his head. ''Forget it. You scare me.''

That tickled her. Even though she doubted that anything scared Nick Grayson.

''What were you like in high school?''

''Like any other kid, I guess. I was a football quarterback in high school and college, and had a chance to go pro.''

''You passed up the opportunity for fame and fortune?'' He was a good four inches over six feet and had shoulders that filled out his suit jacket without the benefit of padding.

''I've got the fortune. And I used my mind to get it, rather than beating up my body. Figured I'd leave the fame for Chase.''

''Ah, driven even as a young man.''

''Thanks,'' he said dryly. ''I needed to feel ancient today.''

She laughed. ''Really, Nick. You should play more. Not take life so seriously.'' They were headed toward the huge ice rink in the mall. Music vied with crying children, giggling shrieks of teens and the noisy hum of shoppers. ''Hey, why don't we go ice skating?''

''I thought you needed shoes.''

''I do. But as long as we're playing hooky from work, we might as well go whole hog. Chicken?''

''Get real. I could skate circles around you. After all, I've had *years* more practice than you.''

''Poked at your ego, did I? Thirty-three is still a young man, Nick. Funny how twelve years ago, the eight-year age difference between us was unacceptable.'' She plucked a green shirt off a sale rack outside a boutique and held it to her chest. ''Now it's not an issue. Why's that?''

''Experience.'' He shook his head, took the shirt out

of her hand and replaced it on the rack. "And until you're eighteen, you're considered jailbait."

"Oh, like my father actually would've had you arrested if you'd kissed me." She hadn't meant to bring up this issue. It had just slipped out. The best thing, she decided, was to simply act sophisticated, as though it was no big deal.

He urged her forward with a hand at her back. "I imagine he would have. And it could have split up the business, as well. Which is why we're not going to continue this conversation."

"Just like that? You say so and it's law?"

"Let's don't go there, Red." He glanced at his watch. "And as much as I'd like to show you up on the ice, I think we'd better tackle those shoes. I need to make a conference call later this afternoon."

"Ever the businessman." She sighed and steered them around the corner, away from the ice rink. "Anything I should know about?"

He hesitated and the look she gave him dared him to put her off again. In the two months she'd been at Coleman-Grayson headquarters she'd never once complained when he'd given her little more responsibility than an office clerk. Instead, she'd taken the opportunity to learn how all the departments ran, from payroll to accounts receivable. She'd worked the switchboard and sat in on planning and investment strategy meetings.

She'd listened and learned—with very little help

from Nick Grayson. She was tired of getting the run-around.

He must have read her determined expression.

''It's a software company I've been looking at. According to the projections, it looks like a solid twenty percent return over the next two years.''

''Software seems so risky right now. Especially competing with the major companies. A lot of start-ups have bitten the dust.''

''This isn't a start-up company. Lusklow's been in business for thirty years with a great track record. The software is a virus-prevention program. They already have a handshake agreement with the Pentagon and a couple of other big players in the industry.''

''You've verified that?''

He glanced down at her as though surprised she'd even ask such a thing. ''Yes. That's part of what the conference call's about.''

''Then I guess we better get cracking on shoes so you can get back in time.''

He looked so relieved that their shopping expedition had an end in sight that she laughed. ''I'd like to listen in on the call, if you don't mind.''

He shrugged. ''Sure. If you want. Coming in on the tail end this way, you probably won't understand some of the technicalities.''

One minute he made her laugh and the next he made her want to slug him. Her mood went from simmer to boil in less than a second. ''Sometimes you make me so mad I could spit.''

"Jess...I didn't mean that the way it sounded."

"Oh, I think you did. One of these days you're going to have to face the fact that I'm not a kid anymore, that I have a brain in my head and a summa cum laude degree to prove it. You're just like every other guy—worse, actually, because you're so darn stuffy about it. You see a big pair of boobs and you think that's all there is to a woman."

He opened his mouth to speak, but she held up her hand and shook her head. Thank God his gaze hadn't wavered from hers. If he'd looked at her chest, she'd have lost it. Big time.

"I'm not in the mood to talk to you right now. You'd be wise to go find a bench somewhere and leave me be while I find some shoes."

Without waiting for him to agree or disagree, she made a beeline for the nearest shoe store, hardly able to see where she was going for the haze of anger that blanked her vision. *Jerk.*

She stewed and fumed and before she knew it, she'd bought ten pairs of shoes and was feeling somewhat better. Nothing like new shoes to set a woman's head on straight.

She'd been handling Nick Grayson all wrong. There were going to be some changes—and soon—or the fur was going to fly. He was bossy, domineering and irritating. She hadn't put up with that kind of behavior from her three macho cousins, and she wouldn't tolerate it with Nick Grayson, either.

As she stood contemplating a pair of sexy little red

sandals in a boutique window, a masculine hand holding an ice-cream cone reached around her.

Her heart lurched, then settled. Despite the nasty words she'd just been calling him in her mind, she smiled, let go of the bags in one hand and plucked the cone out of his. One of the reasons she got along so well with people was that she rarely stayed mad longer than it took to express the emotion.

"Are you bribing me with chocolate, Grayson?"

"Trying to. Is it working?"

She licked the creamy chocolate. "I'll let you know in a minute."

"Jess..." He put a hand on her shoulder, turned her to face him. He held an ice-cream cone in his hand as well—vanilla. "I apologize."

His words and his expression were sincere. Both banished her temper faster than any frozen treat or ten pairs of shoes could.

She took a breath, let it out in a sigh. "Why the heck didn't you say that sooner? Do you know how much money I just spent trying to cool off?"

"I would have said it sooner, but I was afraid you'd inflict harm on my person. I'll never again doubt the cliché about a redhead's temper."

She narrowed her eyes. "Better quit while you're ahead, pal."

"Truce?" he asked.

She laughed. "How long did the other one last?"

"Let's see. It was about two o'clock this morning."

He checked his watch. "That'd make it about twelve hours."

"Practically a record. Wanna make yourself useful and grab a few of these bags?"

"Are we done yet?"

"Yeah, we're done."

"Good. I retrieved the rest of your bags at the hold desk and took them to the car. Any more, and I'll have to rent a truck."

"You're such a sport. Next time, I'll buy the ice cream."

Chapter Three

When they got home from the mall, Jessica remembered to check the messages on her cell phone. Two from her parents and one from Abbie—her college friend and now her cousin Mac's wife—who'd heard about the fire and wanted to check on her.

Nick made several trips carrying in her new wardrobe, then backed out of her bedroom and stood in the hall as though he didn't trust himself to be in the same room with her and a bed.

Attraction? she wondered. Or simply not interested and determined to keep his distance lest she get the wrong impression? Because she wasn't absolutely sure, she became flustered.

''Um, my dad called twice. I guess I better call him back.''

''I thought you said you phoned him this morning.''

''I did. But I got the answering machine.''

Nick stuffed a hand in the pocket of his pants, and his brows drew together. ''You left a message on your parents' answering machine about your apartment burning down? They must be worried sick.''

The censure in his tone annoyed her. ''I left a *detailed,* reassuring message, told them exactly where I was and what I planned to do today in case we missed connecting.'' Criminy, the man even found fault with the way she made a telephone call. ''I think I know how to talk to my own parents, Nick.''

He held up his hands in a gesture of surrender. ''Sorry. I saw the destruction of the fire firsthand. It haunts me.''

Just when her temper was about to soar, he said something to knock the wind out of it. She hadn't thought about what he'd seen conjuring images of horror for him, as well as her.

''Apology accepted and one rendered,'' she said. ''Censure and bossiness pushes my hot button. I spent a lot of years getting my cousins Alex, Cade and Mac to realize I didn't need their guidance, input and overprotective gestures at every turn. I'm a little touchy in that area.''

''Then we're probably going to have a problem. I am who I am, Jess.''

She leaned a shoulder against the doorjamb, grinned when he took another backward step into the hall. ''There's no probably about it, sugar. But if I can train three cowboy sheikhs, it shouldn't be too much of a pain to do the same drill with you.''

''Don't try to handle me, Red.''

''Likewise.''

He stared at her for a long moment, then nodded and turned away. "I'll be in the study."

Jessica moved back into her room and sat on the bed, her legs threatening to give out. Why did sparring with Nick affect her so? Her knees felt like overcooked linguini.

Taking a calming breath, she punched in the number for the Desert Rose Ranch. She half expected the housekeeper, Ella, to answer the phone. Instead, both her parents' voices came over the line, her father's a half a beat after her mother's—obviously from two different extensions.

"Hey, it's me."

"Jessica! Honey, are you all right?" Vi Coleman's voice trembled ever so slightly. She was one of the strongest women Jessica knew. To hear the emotion brought tears to Jess's eyes.

"Didn't you get my message, Mom? I told you everything was fine."

"I know. But I'm a mother. If I can't see and touch one of my children, I imagine the worst—even if you tell me different."

Jessica was Vi's only biological child. But Vi had raised her husband's nephews, Alex, Cade and Mac, from the time they were young boys. Born to Arabian royalty, they'd come to live with their aunt and uncle when danger had threatened their lives. Vi truly considered them her own. And although Aunt Rose was now happily back in their lives after they'd believed her dead all these years, Vi was still the one who held most of the memories of the boys growing up, the one who'd been the main influence in shaping the men they'd become.

"I'm okay, Mom. None of my clothes survived, but I remedied that problem with a trip to the Galleria."

Vi gave a chuckle that ended in a hitch. "I just had the most ridiculous urge to ask if you'd been wearing clean underwear."

Jessica laughed, felt her heart open wide. She was so darn lucky to have such great parents. "Gosh, I love you."

"And we love you," Randy Coleman said, taking over for his wife who seemed to have developed a frog in her throat all of a sudden.

"Hey, Dad." Jess cleared her own throat. "Guess that apartment building is one investment Coleman-Grayson should rethink."

"The insurance company will make it right."

"The building, perhaps, but not the lost rent."

"That's the least of my worries, honey. I'm just thankful you got out unharmed. We saw the photos in the Bridle paper this morning."

"I figured you would. That's why I called early. Where were y'all, anyway?"

"Khalahari had some trouble this morning and we were out in the stable with Alex and Hannah."

"Is she all right?" Jessica knew the highly valuable Arabian mare wasn't due to foal yet. But Khalahari had a history of tough pregnancies and foaling early. Khalid's birth was a prime example. If it hadn't been for Hannah Clark-Coleman, they'd have lost both Khalahari and Khalid. But Hannah, the young veterinarian her cousins had teased as a kid, came through for them all and saved the day. She'd also tempted the sheikh, and now she and Alex were married and the proud parents of four-month-old twin boys.

"Khalahari's fine," Randy said. "It was a false alarm. But you know how Alex is over that mare."

"Mmm."

"I'm glad you're staying with Nick, sweetheart," Vi said. "He'll do right by you."

Jessica wound the phone cord around her finger and refrained from commenting. Her parents had an entirely different perspective of Nick Grayson from hers.

"It shouldn't be for very long. Once I get a car rented—or lease a new one—I'll get out and look for a new place."

"Oh, honey. Don't rush it. Promise me," Vi said. "Stay for a couple of weeks. Your father and I, at least, need that much time to recover our nerves."

Jessica was sure they didn't realize what they were asking of her. Her own nerves might not survive a two-week stay under Nick Grayson's roof. Besides butting heads at nearly every turn, the uncontrollable adrenaline rush of desire she experienced at a mere look or touch was wearing her out.

"Okay, I won't rush off."

"I'm sure you have a hundred things to do, so we won't keep you with any more of our worries. You call if you need us, you hear?" Randy said.

"I'll call, Daddy. And let the rest of the family know that everything here's fine. I love you guys."

She disconnected the call, then dialed the guest house at the Desert Rose, where Abbie and Mac had moved into after they'd married. Might as well take care of all the calls at once.

Twenty minutes later, she still sat on the edge of the bed, her nerves humming from retelling the horror of the fire. She'd played it down of course, but her own vivid memories wouldn't be quieted.

Action was what she needed, she decided, and she got up to put away her new wardrobe. She ought to exercise her independence and go to a hotel. But she'd promised her parents she'd stay with Nick. It made them feel better. Her father was proud of her, truly wanted her to follow in his footsteps, but sometimes he hurt her feelings by insisting she rely on Nick.

Still, she hadn't slept well last night—or rather the hours left of the early morning—because she'd kept seeing smoke and flames and terror every time she'd closed her eyes, hearing the scream of alarms and the wail of sirens.

This house had fire sprinklers hidden in the high ceilings, plenty of windows and doors to get out of in a hurry if the need arose.

And as much as she hated to admit it, she felt better knowing someone else was in the house. Even if he did frustrate the very devil out of her at times.

About to stuff her new black bikini in the drawer, she changed her mind, pulled the tags off and slipped the two pieces on under her sundress. Struggling a bit with the top, she managed to get it in place.

Water had always been a stress reliever for her. Be it the bathtub, shower, a swimming pool or a lake, it revived her.

Carrying her sandals in her hand, she skipped down the richly carpeted staircase and went out the back glass doors. She bypassed the resortlike swimming pool and made her way down the grassy slope of lawn toward the lake.

Clouds gathered in the sky overhead, the humidity hovering at a sticky eighty percent. The unique, familiar smell of the lake surrounded her, wrapping her in a blanket of comfort much the way the smell of freshly baked chocolate-chip cookies evoked warm memories of family gatherings in the kitchen at home on the ranch.

Honestly. She wasn't homesick after only a couple of months. She was just feeling…displaced. That was all.

The boards of the dock that extended out over the water were smooth beneath her feet. Someone had recently slapped a coat of resin over the wood, ensuring bare feet would remain splinter-free.

She glanced longingly at the expensive powerboat, the sun glancing off its white hull. The duel outboards would really make this baby scoot. Jessica loved to go fast—cars, horses, boats. It was so exhilarating, that feeling of being on the edge of danger, free.

Sitting down, she dangled her feet in the cool water,

then pulled her sundress over her head, laid it aside and slipped into the water feetfirst.

She gasped as water closed around her. Warmed by the sun, the first foot or so was deceptive. After that, it was icy cold. Her body adjusted after a couple of minutes and she began to swim, reveling in the way the lake caressed her skin, holding her as she rolled over and floated on her back.

She might have dozed for a minute, but something brushed her leg beneath the water and startled her. Heart jumping, she glanced around, realized it was just a reed tangled around her ankle.

About the time she relaxed again, she looked up and saw Nick coming toward her on the dock.

Carrying a towel.

For some reason, that annoyed her. Oh, sure, she'd forgotten to bring something to dry off with, but the fact that Nick was the one to provide it touched a nerve. Besides, what was wrong with letting a body air-dry in the warm sunshine?

He still wore his suit pants and dress shirt, the sleeves rolled up to his elbows, exposing tanned, muscular forearms. Didn't the guy believe in getting comfortable?

"The swimming pool too civilized for you?" he asked.

She treaded water, looking up at him. The sun was behind his head, making it difficult to see his expression. She imagined he had a fine view of her, though.

"Lake water's much nicer to my skin. Besides, it's

what I'm used to. I swim in the lake at the Desert Rose, so this feels like home."

He crouched down, shifting out of the direct sunlight so she didn't have to squint. Or wonder what expression he wore.

The traditional scowl. Figured.

It bothered her even more that those rigid scowls turned her on. Sheesh.

She reached up for the edge of the dock, afraid she'd drown herself with the way this man affected her limbs and her breathing.

"Want a hand?" he asked.

"I'm good, thanks." She saw his gaze dip to her cleavage. Heck, even if she ducked her shoulders under the water, he'd still be able to see through the clear lake water. She'd churned up the water just enough to have it lapping softly against the dock, each buoyant ripple gently lifting her breasts.

And he still looked.

Honestly. Talk about ruining all the benefits of the stress-relief swim. "On second thought, maybe I will—"

Before she could finish her sentence or advise him to step back so he wouldn't get wet, he hooked his hands beneath her arms and lifted her out of the water as though she weighed little more than a leather saddle.

She grabbed for his arms, then flattened her palms on his chest to steady herself on her feet, leaving wet handprints on his upper arms and front of his shirt.

"Criminy. Warn a person, why don't you." She

reached for the towel, dabbed at the water on herself, then dabbed at his shirt.

He stepped back. "I'll dry."

"Well, it serves you right. I could have gotten out just fine by myself and saved you a change of clothes—though why you're still wearing your business clothes is beyond me."

"Jessica?"

"What?" She blotted her face and chest with the towel, held it in front of her.

A dimple winked in one of his cheeks. He picked up the end of the towel, dabbed at her jaw. "You missed a spot."

She could hardly draw a breath, much less speak. After standing frozen like a dummy for a full three seconds, she snatched the towel back from him and wrapped it around her torso, covering herself from chest to knees. "Thank you. I can get the rest."

He stepped back and shoved his hands back in his pockets. "Do I make you nervous?"

"Of course not." *Absolutely.*

"Then how come you get that little twitch beside your eye when I get close?"

"Annoyance, probably."

His lips curved ever so slightly. "I came out to tell you I'll be placing that conference call to the West Coast in twenty minutes."

"Oh. Thank you for reminding me. I'll be right in."

"You've got time still." He turned, started to walk away, then paused. "Hey, Red?"

She'd just picked up the edge of the towel to blot her hair. "Yes?"

"I like your suit. It's, uh…sexy."

She dropped her arm and the corner of the towel she'd lifted, her jaw going slack when he winked.

Doggone it, she was going to figure this man out, learn to keep her emotions on an even keel around him. Otherwise, the way her heart kept leaping, she'd have a heart attack at the ripe young age of twenty-five.

On the other hand…sexy was much better than the bland "nice" he'd uttered over the red dress at the mall. It was definitely better than "kiddo." And calling her Red…now that was about as unoriginal as you could get when faced with a woman like her with bright red hair.

In all honesty, she kind of liked the nickname. It was friendly, more intimate. Much better than kiddo, that was for sure, though not as good as darling or sweetheart or…

Criminy! Get a grip!

FIVE MINUTES BEFORE the scheduled call, Jessica knocked lightly on the open door of the study and went in when Nick gestured her forward. He was speaking on the phone, and since the conversation sounded like a personal one, she wandered around the room.

She trailed her fingers over dark, rich woods, oversize, comfortable furniture and shelves of books. On the wall was a photo of Nick's brother, Chase, at the helm of a sailboat, and another one of him holding a trophy beside a race car. There were several poses of his parents, as well as pictures of beautiful Arabian horses that she knew for certain had come from Desert Rose stock.

For a guy who seemed to be all work and little play, the pictures on the walls painted him as a family man. There were none of the priceless, stuffy art pieces that a lot of wealthy people treasured. Instead, the paneling was adorned with images of his parents, his brother and the sleek Arabians he loved. Interesting.

She shoved a stray curl off her forehead. Her hair was still damp from her swim, so she'd pinned it in a loose knot on top of her head. She saw Nick's gaze pass over her, saw his frown and could just imagine what he was thinking—that a barefoot woman in a short sundress wasn't his idea of a businesswoman to be taken seriously.

But honestly. She wasn't about to put on panty hose, a suit and heels just to listen to a business meeting over the speaker phone. This was one of the things that annoyed her—being judged by appearance.

Before she could get totally carried away putting thoughts in his head that, in all fairness, might not be there, he hung up the phone and leaned back in the chair.

"Change of plans. The CEO at Lusklow had an illness in the family to attend to."

"Oh, I hope everything's all right."

"Yeah, me, too. They suspect his wife has cancer.

He's dropping everything and staying home with her until they get word."

"I like him already."

Nick raised a brow. "That surprises you—that a man would put his family ahead of business?"

"No. It doesn't surprise me. I just said I *liked* that about him. The men in my family put their personal lives above business. It's what I'm used to."

She sat down on a leather chair, felt the dampness of her bathing suit seep through onto the back of her sundress. Great. Now she'd have to find a way to back out of the room without looking like a total dork.

"You'll learn that I generally do business only with people I like and respect."

"Are you saying if a company came to you with a surefire moneymaking proposition, no way to lose, and you didn't like the major players, you'd turn down the opportunity?"

"Yes. There are plenty of deals out there."

"Do you ever run into a situation where somebody doesn't like *you?*"

"Sure. Same holds true. If we can't get along, no sense mingling our business."

Jessica wondered if that "we" was actually aimed at her. Heck, they could hardly sustain a truce for twelve hours. And they were already business partners.

That worried her. Was there room at the top of Coleman-Grayson for both of them? Their personalities were totally different from their fathers. Just because Jared Grayson and Randy Coleman meshed as a team didn't mean Nick and Jessica would. Their fathers had formed a partnership based on like ideas—and had chosen each other.

Nick and Jessica were tossed into the arena by birth, not forethought.

All around, this could be a risky thing.

Though it was a risk Jessica was willing to take.

After graduation, she'd put off coming to work in Dallas, sure that she'd miss the ranch. But as her cousins got married and their wives became more active in the horse-ranching business, Jess had begun to feel out of the loop.

That was probably just the push she'd needed, because she'd realized immediately that working at Coleman-Grayson in the city appealed to a reckless, hungry side of her she'd always known was there but never fully trusted or given rein to.

She loved every facet of the corporate world she'd been introduced to so far.

Now if she could just get Nick Grayson to get with the program and give her more responsibility, she could set about sating that hunger.

First, though, she needed to finish putting the pieces of her charred life back in order. Starting with wheels. She'd promised her folks she'd stay at Nick's for a couple of weeks. She wasn't going to rely on him for transportation, too.

"Well, since the afternoon is so conveniently freed up, I think I'll go change and call a cab to—"

"What do you need with a cab?" he interrupted. "I've got plenty of cars."

She laughed. "That sounds really snooty. Cars plural. Shame on you."

"What's wrong with having more than one car?"

"Nothing, I guess. But since I don't have even one at the moment, I need to hit the dealership and remedy that. Then I thought I'd drive by the apartment building and see if there's anything left of my stuff."

"First off, you should lease a car in the company's name. So I'll need to go with you."

She kept a lid on her temper. It was an effort.

"You forget that I'm a board member and major stockholder. I think I can lease a car on my own signature. However, if you want to stand by my side and do your big-scary-guy scowling thing, that's fine by me. It'll save me from having to haggle so hard with the salesman." There. She'd spoken pleasantly enough.

He ran a hand over his forehead, right where the crease showed his emotions, and spoke as though she hadn't said a word. "Second, I don't think you should go back to the apartment yet. I doubt the fire officials have finished going over the scene."

"Strike two, Grayson."

"Excuse me?"

"I'm well past the age of being told what I can and can't or should and shouldn't do. We've covered this ground before, you and me, and it dismays me to have to repeat the lesson—*every* few minutes, I might add."

He stared at her as though she'd grown an extra

head. Then he shook his head and the corner of his lips twitched. ''Did your cousins actually put up with this sass?''

She grinned. ''Absolutely. So, hey. If royalty can get in line, so can you.''

He bowed like a commoner before a queen. ''Very well, Ms. Coleman. I shall be out front by the car, awaiting your instructions.''

She laughed. ''Now that's what I like. A guy who's a quick study. There might be hope for you yet.''

His eyes narrowed, but amusement showed through. ''Don't push your luck, Red.''

Chapter Four

By the time Jessica collapsed into bed that night, she was tired to the bone, on edge, and surprisingly she fell instantly asleep.

But instead of pleasant dreams…

She moaned. The smoke was so thick. It burned her throat, snatched her breath. There was no air to breathe. She tried to inhale, but her chest hurt. She was smothering, could hardly see.

But she needed to see. It was important.

Oh, God! Glass exploded and metal twisted with a sickening groan.

The roof was coming down on them.

She had to get out. *Run!*

But someone was crying, calling for Boots. Timmy. He'd lost his cat again. He usually used that as an excuse to knock on Jessica's door, knowing she'd invite him in for cookies and milk, then help him find his orange-and-white tabby.

No, that wasn't right. Those weren't small knuckles

knocking on the door. It was the popping of drywall screws as metal separated from gypsum.

And Timmy was crying.

She ran into the hall, panting, feeling as though she was moving in slow motion. Why wouldn't her legs go faster? The floor was hot, burning her toes beneath the flimsy soles of her sandals.

People pushed and shoved toward the exits. Fire alarms screamed, further promoting hysteria.

Frantically she looked around. And then she saw him.

"Timmy, wait! You're going the wrong way! Oh, God, don't open that door!" Smoke bellowed from the slit at the bottom of the door that led to the basement. Like a monster lurking, sinister flames licked at the other side of the door, waiting for a cool draft of air so it could spread its devil's breath and destroy.

She reached for the back of Timmy's shirt. He tripped. No! Oh, no! She couldn't reach him. She couldn't—

"Jessica! Come on, Jess. Wake up now."

Her eyes popped open. Her heart was pounding. Sweat plastered her tank top to her chest. Her arms were slick with moisture.

"That's right, Red. You're safe now."

Slowly, ever so slowly, her vision focused. Nick sat on the edge of her bed, his chest bare, his hands incredibly gentle as he stroked the damp hair back from her forehead.

"A dream," she said, her throat dry and scratchy as though she'd actually been breathing smoke. Had she screamed? The images were so vivid, felt so real. "I'm sorry."

"Shh. Want a drink of water?"

She nodded and he got off the bed and went to the bathroom. She heard the water running. Still disoriented, she looked around and realized that her bedside lamp was on.

Embarrassment swamped her. She hadn't woken from a nightmare since she was nine years old and had seen Tori Newman mauled by a dog. For weeks, every time she'd closed her eyes, she'd seen sharp teeth and torn flesh, seen her best friend clamped in the snarling jaws of a huge black animal and shaken like a rag doll.

Nightmares were for kids. Not grown women.

Nick came back to the bed and handed her a glass of water.

"Thanks." She scooted over a bit to give him room to sit and sipped the cool liquid. "I'm fine. Sorry I woke you." She laughed, then swallowed the sound when it seemed on the verge of turning into a sob.

"The fire?" he asked, stroking her hair behind her ears.

"Yes."

"You were calling out for Timmy."

She set the water glass on the nightstand, unsure what to do with her hands. The bare skin of his chest was so close, his hip pressed against her thigh. She could hardly think.

"He's the little boy who lived next door. Six years old, a real cutie. His cat, Boots, didn't much like being cooped up in an apartment and was forever wandering.''

She swallowed hard and Nick rubbed a soothing palm over her leg, which was covered by a crisp cotton sheet and lightweight blanket.

''The fire was climbing the walls like clear orange vapor. I've never seen anything like that. Timmy was trying to go back to look for the cat. His mom had her hands full with the baby and her husband, Tony. Tony's leg was in a cast. I told them to go on, that I'd get Timmy.

''Then I saw him fall, heard him scream as a flame shot out and slapped his fingers. His little hand was burned. I didn't know what to do. I knew we had to get out of there. I picked him up, but he begged me to wait, to not leave without Boots.''

She put her hands over her face, drew her knees up. ''I carried him out and he fought me all the way. The accusation in his eyes ripped my heart out.''

''Shh.'' Nick drew her hands away from her face, put his arms around her and held her to his chest. ''You did the right thing, Red.''

''I know.'' She sniffed. ''Stupid cat was already outside.''

''Figures. He probably used up one of his nine lives.''

She chuckled against his shoulder. ''Probably.''

He held her and rubbed her back. Jessica knew she should pull away, but her nerves were too frayed. Just a minute more, she promised herself. His skin felt warm and smooth beneath her hands, his shoulders wide enough to carry a great load.

Not that she wanted him to carry a load for her. But it was nice to feel the gentle companionship for once, the easy comfort.

"I shouldn't have let you go back to look at the apartment tonight."

She went still. So much for a good thing lasting.

She leaned back against the pillows. "Nobody *lets* me do things, Nick. In case you hadn't noticed, I'm a grown woman. I make my own choices."

"Well, damn it, you made a bad one."

"Criminy, what are you getting so worked up about? It was *my* nightmare."

He stood up and she realized he was only wearing his underwear. Boxer shorts that covered all the strategic parts, but still...how had she missed this detail?

When he turned around, glared at her with his hands on his hips, she swallowed a bubble of laughter. Evidently not successfully enough.

"Is something funny?"

She shrugged and bit her bottom lip. "Um, I think we're having our first argument in our underwear."

He glanced down at himself, took a deep breath and relaxed his stance. "You're hell on a man's ego, Red. Women don't usually laugh at my skivvies."

Her heart started a slow deep pound. For once he was actually looking at her the way a man looks at a woman. Not a kid.

And she was in a bed.

And both of them were in their underclothes.

"Um, sorry."

He looked at her for a long moment, his gaze skimming over her hair, her lips, her chest. "Want me to turn out the light?"

"I can get it."

"Okay, then." He moved toward the door, hesitated.

Jessica held her breath. Her lips actually tingled as she imagined what it would be like to kiss him. Really kiss him without him pushing her away and calling her a spoiled little girl, threatening to turn her over his knee.

That had been the most humiliating part of his rejection. His acting like a father or something. Heck, he was eight years old when she was born. Hardly old enough to be her father.

"Jess?"

"Yes?"

"I *did* notice." He left the room, closing the door behind him.

In case you hadn't noticed, I'm a grown woman.

Jessica let out the breath she'd been holding, scooted down in bed and hugged the pillow. She felt like weeping.

"That was a fine time to say something like that and just walk out the door, Grayson," she muttered. "Especially when I'm not at my best."

She punched the pillow, flopped over onto her back.

She had no business fantasizing about kissing Nick Grayson. He was arrogant, bossy, demanding and stuffy.

He wasn't the right man for her.

She had to find neutral ground with him in order for them to work together. But that was it.

She closed her eyes. Lord, but the man had a nice body. Brains, too, but at the moment that fact seemed less important.

Groaning, she pulled the pillow over her face. Now, instead of feeling weepy, she felt like screaming.

Nick Grayson could frustrate the horns off a billy goat.

AT WORK SEVERAL DAYS later, Jessica couldn't believe the difference in Nick. Where was the charming pal who'd shopped with her? The guy who'd bought her ice cream and apologized so sincerely? The gentle man who'd held her in the middle of the night when a nightmare had gripped her?

He was back to his split-personality routine, avoiding her.

The man was an enigma.

At least he was spending more time in the office—albeit with his door closed.

Well, she'd made up her mind that there would be changes, and she was going to see to it. She'd put off going to work for the company—mainly because of Nick Grayson. Then she'd wised up and realized she was basically cutting off her nose to spite her face.

She had a degree in business and finance, had known from the time she was young that she someday wanted to make her own mark on the world—mainly through Coleman-Grayson Investment Company.

So here she was, in the fancy high-rise building in

Dallas, and up until recently Nick had hardly shown his face around the office, let alone taught her the ropes.

It was as though he didn't respect her as a worthy partner, was biding his time until she picked up her toys and went home.

"Well, don't hold your breath, pal," she muttered, and got up from her desk to make her way to Nick's closed office door.

And what was the matter with her lately? She didn't like the man—most of the time—could hardly have a civil conversation with him, yet one glimpse of his dark hair, broad shoulders, sexy, self-assured walk, and she suddenly had trouble catching her breath.

Her mind and hormones were annoyingly out of sync.

Besides, the last person she should be attracted to was a man who didn't have a clue that she actually had a brain.

Maybe that was partly her fault. She'd developed early, and boys had taken notice. To hold them at bay, she'd perfected an aloof seductress act that effectively scared guys off.

She'd done it so often it had become a habit. Then she would inevitably reflect back on her behavior and feel empty.

She wanted to be accepted for who she was inside, not just voluptuous breasts and pouty lips—and eyes of two different colors.

Lord that was the worst. Every guy she'd ever met

had used some corny line about her eyes. Nobody was original these days.

Perhaps she should give Nick points. *He'd* never commented on them.

''Is he with anyone?'' she asked the secretary, whose desk was in the outer office.

''Not at the moment,'' Rhonda said. ''Want me to buzz him?''

''That's okay. Surprise visits will keep a man on his toes.''

Rhonda chuckled. ''Be warned. He's in a weird mood.''

''So what else is new?'' She knocked on Nick's door and politely waited to be invited in. His tone was less than cordial when he bade her entrance, but that didn't stop her.

He looked up from the paperwork in front of him. That permanent crease in his forehead deepened even more as he realized who'd just breached his sanctuary. His dark hair looked nearly black where it brushed the collar of a stark-white business shirt. His silk tie was a blend of gray and maroon, a perfect choice for the gray suit jacket hanging on the coatrack in the corner.

The epitome of a high-powered businessman.

A businessman with more than his fair share of good looks.

She pulled up a chair and sat down, raising a brow at the mess on his desk.

''A bit disorganized, aren't we? I don't suppose you need some help with that?''

He tilted back in his chair and raked his fingers through his hair. "I'm kind of busy here, Jess."

"Then I'll get right to the point. I want more responsibility, accounts of my own. In fact, I've been doing research on some breeding farms. I know for a fact that they're lucrative business—"

"Not always."

"Doggone it! Can't you just hush up and listen for a minute?"

He gave a shrug of surrender. "Go ahead."

"Nick, I know my way backward and forward around a horse and everything that goes into breeding farms. Did you forget how this partnership started twenty-five years ago? The Desert Rose is what brought our fathers together in the first place."

"I know the story, Jess."

"Okay, then. Oil, textile and software companies are all well and good, but there are other markets to be tapped."

"And you want to tap them."

"Is there anything wrong with that?"

"Ambition's a fine trait. But a person usually crawls before they walk."

"Damn it, I've been crawling since I stepped foot in these offices! I could probably run this company better than you do."

"You think so?"

"Do you know how to write a payroll check? When the taxes are due? Could you operate that switchboard out in reception if you had to? I doubt it," she said before he could answer. "But I can. While you've been avoiding this place since I came, I've been learning all the little details about how it's run. The overhead expenses and behind-the-scenes stuff that's the glue that holds any successful company together."

"A good businessman knows how to delegate."

"Yes. And a good businessperson knows all the ins and outs of what he delegates."

"Touché." He pulled a couple of folders out of his desk drawer and tossed them toward her. "See what you think of these, what changes you'd make, and give me a report."

She grinned and pounced on the folders, then stood and saluted. "Right away, sir."

Although the frowning crease in his forehead remained, his lips twitched.

"See, that wasn't so hard, was it?" she asked sweetly, and headed toward the door, anxious to get started.

"Jess?"

She paused. "Yes?"

"My folks want us to come to dinner tonight."

"Us?"

He sighed. "Yeah, us. They said I wasn't to show up unless you were with me."

"Why?"

"Don't ask me. I think your mother and mine have been scaring each other with *what ifs* over the fire. Mom said it's a family dinner and you're family."

She grinned. "Okay, I'll see if I can clear my social calendar." He didn't appear thrilled that his mother considered her family. Silly, really. Her own family treated Nick like one of theirs. He came to all the weddings and get-togethers.

No reason she couldn't enjoy a little time in the company of his parents and brother.

Hugging the folders to her chest, she wagged her fingers at him in farewell.

"One more thing, Jess." When she turned back toward him, he said, "I haven't been avoiding this place."

Jessica cocked her head and gave him a smile filled with enough wattage to melt steel. She knew she'd hit her target when his fingers went slack around his gold Cross pen.

"Nick Grayson, you lie like a dog." Laughing, she let herself out of his office.

Three hours later, she wasn't smiling. In fact, she was having a great deal of trouble keeping a lid on her emotions.

He'd given her two Coleman-Grayson companies to handle—both were losing money hand over fist and were a few steps away from bankruptcy.

Darn his hide, he'd set her up to fail.

Well, that wasn't going to happen. Mr. Stuffed Shirt was going to have to eat his smirk.

Chapter Five

At five-thirty that afternoon, Jessica had just reached the turnoff for Nick's driveway when her cell phone rang. She picked up the palm-size unit, glanced at the caller ID and tossed the phone back in her purse.

"Jerk," she muttered. Nick's name and telephone number were scrolled across the ID window of her phone.

She let it ring.

The double security gates were standing open as she turned onto the long concrete drive. White wood fences bordered both sides, and strategically spaced oaks cast long shadows in the late-afternoon sun. Horses grazed on expansive verdant lawns.

The sight was almost enough to soothe her.

Almost.

When she pulled her red Chevy Tahoe under the porte-cochere, the phone abruptly stopped ringing and Nick stepped out the front door.

He looked about as happy as she was. And *she* could probably make a hornet look cuddly.

She lowered the window on the passenger side.

"Why didn't you answer your phone?" he demanded.

"No sense. I was right down the road."

"Did you forget we were supposed to be at my parents for dinner?"

"I'm here, aren't I? Get in."

He frowned. "My car's already out."

"And mine's running. Are we going to argue, take two cars, or are you going to get the heck in?"

He got in and slammed the door behind him. Before he'd gotten his seat belt buckled, Jessica put the car in gear and punched the gas.

"We were supposed to be there at five-thirty," he said as he shot the buckle home and made a grab for the dash.

"So, we'll be five minutes late. I'm sure they're used to that with you."

"Why the hell does everything have to be a battle with us?"

She shrugged and turned out onto the highway. "Beats me."

"And what's wrong with you, anyway?"

"As if you didn't know." She reached over and turned up the radio.

He switched the station.

She started to turn it back just for spite, but she liked the Faith Hill song that was playing and left it alone.

"You're going to pass the turnoff."

"I know where your parents live, Nick." She nearly grinned as his knuckles turned white on the dash.

"I bet you don't know that Deke Grover likes to hide out in his patrol car right behind that big sycamore on Bloody Bucket Road."

"Heck, with a name like that, I'd expect the law to keep a watch on it." She eased off the gas to make the turn—not because he'd worried her with the threat of getting a ticket. "You want to be later than we already are?"

"I'd like to arrive shiny side up. And who's fault is it that we're late, anyway?"

"Yours." She pulled into the driveway of the Graysons' home. It was a fine old estate with lovely grounds and an Old World charm about it. The kind of place that made one want to sit on a porch swing and just enjoy the day.

"Mine? *I* was already home."

She turned off the car, got out and slung her purse over her shoulder. She was still wearing the summer suit she'd worn to work, except she'd taken off the jacket. The silk shell tucked into the waistband of her above-the-knee skirt was sticking to her skin in the humidity.

She rounded the hood of the car and met him at the steps. They didn't have time to continue sniping at each other because Gloria Grayson had already opened the front double doors.

"Well, I see nothing's changed here." Gloria looked from her oldest son to Jessica. "Isn't it comforting to know there are certain things we can always count on?"

Chase came up behind her. "You count on Nick and Jess to stare daggers at each other? That's not very sporting of you, Mom."

"Why, I don't know what you mean. I was merely referring to—"

"It's okay, Gloria," Jessica interrupted before the woman was forced to tell a fib. "I forgive you for raising such an ornery son. Now with this one," she said, reaching up to give Chase a peck on the cheek, "you did an excellent job. Not an argumentative bone in his body."

"Compliments," Chase said with a wink. "I love them."

Nick bent down to give his mother a kiss on the cheek.

"Nicholas, have you been giving Jessica a hard time?"

"Why does it always have to be my fault?" he muttered. "Did you ever think she might be tough on me?"

He might as well have been talking to himself, because Gloria ignored him when her husband came into the room.

"Well, look who's here," Jared Grayson said, ambling into the foyer as though he had time on his hands and intended to enjoy every second of it. He wore a white bib apron that bore a slogan claiming he was the best cook in Texas. "Come in, you two. I've got a hell of a barbecue going out back."

"Armadillo?" Jess asked.

It was a joke between them. Jared had teased her when she was a child, telling her the venison steak was the old armadillo that trotted across the yard every evening. Since it was the first time she'd ever tasted venison, she'd believed him.

Nick had actually been the one to tell her the truth when she'd touched her tongue to the meat and shivered.

"Best armadillo in the state." Jared put his arm around her and led her through the house. "Man alive, when did you grow up on me, girl?"

"A long time ago, Mr. G."

"Is our boy, here, treating you right? Catching you up to speed on all the goings-on at the office?"

"Oh, absolutely." She shot Nick a smile that should have knocked him flat on his butt. "Why, just today he turned over two long-standing accounts to me. I can't tell you how it makes me feel to be entrusted with so much responsibility. And so soon."

"Soon, my foot. You were accepting responsibility when you were knee-high to a grasshopper. Sit down, sweet thing, and get a load off your mind. Your mama and daddy have been as worried as a couple of camels in the Klondike."

Jessica sat on the padded glider swing and kicked off her shoes. The smell of mesquite smoke filled the air, as well as the faint aroma of chlorine from the rushing waterfall that emptied into the pool.

Those nasty insects were already singing in the trees.

"I swear those peepers deliberately get louder when I come outside," she said, keeping an eye on the elm tree that was stretching its branches toward the patio.

"Give you the willies, do they?" Jared asked with a laugh.

"Oh, I'm glad to know I'm not the only one who shivers at those silly bugs," Gloria said as she brought a tray of lemonade out onto the patio. Chase followed with a plate of cheese and crackers. "Nick, sit down beside Jessica."

"I'm fine, Mom."

She gave him a stern look. He shrugged and grabbed two glasses of lemonade off the tray, then sat down, handing one of the glasses to Jessica.

"Thank you," she murmured, and took a sip to hide her grin. It did her heart good to see this tough guy being bossed by his mother, a woman who stood barely as tall as his shoulder.

Interesting how Nick could glare daggers at her and still thoughtfully hand her a drink as though she were his date and he did it all the time. She didn't even think he was aware of the gentlemanly act.

Chase slouched in a patio chair and didn't bother to hide his taunting smile. "I'd have been glad to sit by Jess."

"Of course you would, sweetheart," Gloria said, and dropped a kiss on the top of her younger son's blond head. "But you'll sit by me, instead, because it's been so long since I've seen you."

"Well, now I'm insulted," Nick said with a mock glare at his brother. "I always knew she loved you best."

"Oh, hush and mind your manners." The proud twinkle in Gloria Grayson's eyes clearly stated that *both* sons were her absolute heart.

Jessica watched the byplay between the Graysons and caught glimpses of another side of Nick.

The relaxed side.

Conversation flowed easily and lovingly between them. This was the guy whom everyone else liked and got along with so well.

Evidently she was the only one who brought out his overbearing side.

Nick took a sip of lemonade and glanced down at Jessica. She'd fallen silent, and from the faraway look in her eyes, he didn't think she was aware his mother had spoken to her.

"You asleep?" he murmured, lightly touching his elbow to hers.

She glanced at him for a moment—just long enough to make him sweat at the sight of those pouty lips so close to his—then looked away.

"I'm sorry, Gloria. Did you say something to me?"

"I asked if you were able to salvage anything from the fire."

"Mom, I don't think Jess wants to go into that," Nick said. "She's already having nightmares." He noticed that she was rubbing a scar on her index finger. He remembered the dog-attack incident. His parents had told him about it, and they'd all worried about her because it had taken so long for her to get over her nightmares.

At nine years old, she'd disregarded peril to herself and dove in to save her little friend from the jaws of a dog. Just as she'd gone back for Timmy without a thought for her own safety.

Jessica was about as loyal and brave as they came.

"Oh, honey," Gloria said, "can I do anything to help?"

Jessica glared at Nick and he stared right back. He won that match and she looked away.

"It's not as bad as Nick's making out. I wasn't in danger."

Nick snorted.

"And no, I wasn't able to salvage anything—except my family pictures. I had the presence of mind to grab them on my way out. Besides, I hadn't lived there long enough to get emotionally attached or fill the place with keepsakes."

"Still, it's a devastating fright," Jared commented, opening the barrel lid of the barbecue, letting out a billow of thick white smoke.

Nick reached over and placed his hand on top of Jessica's. "Maybe a barbecue wasn't such a good idea." He said it only loud enough for her to hear.

She smiled at him, surprising him because it was genuine. "You're a worrywart. Why don't you pass me that plate of cheese and crackers before I faint from hunger?"

Nick figured he was the one about to faint from hunger. And not for cheese and crackers.

The moist contours of Jessica's lips made a craving inside him sit up and howl.

LIBBY, THE GRAYSONS' longtime housekeeper, shooed Jessica out of the kitchen, insisting that guests didn't do dishes.

Jessica tried to object. After all, the Colemans had a housekeeper, too, but that didn't stop Jess from pitching in and helping Ella tidy up.

Knowing she was on the losing end of the battle, she went into the living room and wandered around. Chase and Nick were helping their father shift some boxes in the garage, and Gloria had excused herself to go upstairs to the powder room.

Jess hadn't been to the Graysons often. They'd always come to the Desert Rose to visit and conduct business. She smiled at the army of photographs on the enormous fireplace mantel. Like Nick, his parents also displayed family pictures as art.

There were baby pictures of the boys, graduation photos from high school and college, birthday parties…

She frowned and stepped closer, lifting a five-by-seven wood frame off the mantel. The photo had been taken at the Desert Rose.

It was her thirteenth birthday.

Nick had been twenty-one. He had his arm around her, and both were smiling into the camera. She'd been wearing shorts and a purple top that showed off her early-developing body.

She remembered the fresh smell of laundry detergent on his T-shirt, remembered the way her young heart had pounded at the feel of his strong body so close to hers.

That was the day she'd gotten the crazy idea he could be interested in her.

She sucked in a breath. My gosh, she was just a little girl.

And he'd been a man.

It was so obvious in the photo, the images showing her what her young girl's heart had refused to see.

"Reminiscing?"

She jumped like a scalded cat at the sound of Nick's voice just behind her. Slowly she turned, still holding the framed photograph in her hands.

"Now I get it." Her voice was hushed. "I was too young for you."

He seemed to know exactly what she was talking about, and his expression softened. "Or I was too old for you."

She glanced down at the picture. "Either way, I hated you for what you did. You rejected me and it hurt so bad."

"I know. If I could go back and do it over, I would." He reached out as though he would touch her, then dropped his hand. "I'd be gentler."

She shook her head. "I doubt it would have made any difference. I put you in an awkward position." She never thought she'd be saying these words to Nick Grayson. "I'm sorry."

His gaze dipped to her mouth, and Jessica's heart tripped. She'd just apologized to the man for putting him in an awkward position, yet here she stood, yearning once again to kiss him.

"Dessert," Gloria called, china rattling against silver as she carried a tray laden with goodies into the room. Jared and Chase were right behind her.

Jessica whirled around and put the photo back on the mantel. Saved by his mother, she thought. She hoped to heaven no one had noticed she'd been a split second away from having *Nick* for dessert.

This time, Jessica didn't give Gloria Grayson the opportunity to seat Nick next to her. She chose an overstuffed chair and sat down.

"Libby made her famous pecan pie," Gloria said as she poured coffee into cups and passed around plates.

Jessica noticed that Nick was watching her as she accepted the piece of pie. Well, honestly. Maybe he was used to being around twigs who declined dessert in favor of their figures, but she wasn't one of them.

A sane person simply did not pass up Libby's pecan pie.

After everyone sat down and had moaned appreciatively over the dessert, Gloria set her cup on the table. "How is your aunt Rose, dear?"

"Mom," Chase said, censure in his voice.

Everyone looked at him as though he'd shouted a curse word. Then Jessica remembered.

"I forgot, you've been out of the country. A lot has happened in the last couple of years."

The Graysons all knew that Jessica's cousins, Alex, Cade and Mac had been born to Arabian royalty, but were ripped from their home when their father—the king of their country—was murdered. Rose, the boys' mother and Jessica's father's sister, believed the boys were in danger, so she'd contacted her brother and asked him to care for them. She'd brought them to America, then returned to Sorajhee to try to expose the person who'd killed her husband, promising to come back for the boys when she'd completed her mission.

But she'd never made it back. The Colemans had received word that Rose had died. And that was when Randy had moved his family from Boston to Texas and entered into a partnership with Jared Grayson.

"Aunt Rose is doing great, Gloria." Jessica turned her attention to Chase. "We found out that she hadn't died, after all. Her sister-in-law had her put in a sanatorium in France. Evidently Layla—the sister-in-law—wanted to be queen and was the one who ordered the death of Rose's husband, Ibrahim. She pretended to be Rose's confidant, then had Rose committed."

"Heavy stuff," Chase said.

"That's only the tip of it. Rose was pregnant at the time—and nobody knew. Except Layla of course. When Rose had the fourth son—Sharif—he was taken away from her at birth and given to the king of Balahar to raise."

"The king with the mean wife?"

Jessica laughed. "No. Ibrahim, who died, was the brother of Layla's husband, Azzam, who took over as king of Sorajhee. The neighboring country that's been trying to form an alliance all these years is Balahar. Zak—actually Zakariyya Bin Kamil Al Farid—was the king of Balahar. He's the one who figured out that his adopted son, Sharif, was Rose's. He contacted Aunt Rose, fell head over heels in love with her, and now they're married." Oh, she loved telling this story. It was like a fairy tale.

"And Zakariyya's adopted goddaughter married your cousin Cade," Jared said.

"Yes. Goes to show what a small world this is," Jessica said. "Chase, you already knew that Alex married Hannah Clark—the vet?"

"Yeah, I did know that."

"Well, they have four-month-old twin boys now. Ryan and Justin. And Mac ended up marrying my college friend, Abbie Jones. They have a baby girl, Sarah Rose Coleman El-Jeved."

"Happy endings," Gloria said with a sigh. "Don't you just love them?"

Jessica got the oddest feeling that something was up. The way Nick's mother looked at the two of them as she extolled happy endings seemed to convey more than just a casual comment.

Surely they weren't thinking...

No, Jessica decided. Anyone who'd been around them for more than five minutes knew that Jess and Nick weren't twosome material.

Both Nick and Chase looked equally uncomfortable at the expression of yearning on their mother's face. Jessica almost laughed.

Chase stood up. "Well, since this night's not at an end yet, what do you say we play a game of pool, Jess? Work up an appetite so we can have another piece of Libby's excellent pie." He gallantly held out his hand to help her up.

Nick stood, as well. He didn't know where this pang of annoyance came from, but just looking at his younger brother's blond playboy looks and charming grin set him on edge. He told himself he was simply being the one to keep a level head.

After all, he couldn't blame his brother for being taken with Jessica. Any man with half a pulse and a pair of eyes would respond to the siren call of all that energy encased in such a dynamite body.

Jessica was the type of woman whose charisma could turn a perfectly intelligent man into an adoringly stupid puppy in a matter of minutes.

"It's a work night, bro," Nick said. "Jess and I should probably head home."

Chase raised his brows at the same time Jessica and his parents all looked at their watches.

Nick felt like a nerd.

"It's hardly eight o'clock, dear," Gloria said. "Are you not getting enough sleep?"

No, he damned well wasn't. Not since Jessica Coleman had moved into his life and taken over his thoughts.

For as much as she'd occupied his thoughts over the years, it was a wonder he wasn't comatose by now.

"I'll make a deal," Jessica said. "The minute I lose a game, we'll go."

Nick and Chase had grown up playing pool. They were both better than good. He figured they'd be home by eight-thirty.

"Fair enough."

He watched Chase and Jessica tease each other as they racked the balls and flipped a coin to see who would break. Both his brother and Jessica laughed so easily, took such delight in the smallest things.

Had Nick himself ever been that carefree?

Jessica ran her fingers lovingly over the cue stick, making him sweat. Then she leaned down to check the level of the table, sliding the smooth wood of the stick through her fingers in a way that made him hard. He'd been playing pool all his life, and never once had he been turned on by the way someone held the cue, never once viewed it as a sensual act.

Hell, he was probably more tired than he'd thought. Jessica's nightmare had interrupted his sleep. Sparring with her for a good portion of the rest of the day had been taxing. That was all there was to it.

Her short skirt hugged her thighs, making him wish it would give way and ride up a bit farther when she bent that way. She was still barefoot, and the cream silk shell she wore had enough slack to give everyone in the room a modest, yet teeth-clenching view of her cleavage.

She wasn't deliberately being provocative or exploiting herself. She was a combination of classy casual, at ease with herself. She was quick to laugh and easy to keep a conversation going with.

And all that glorious red hair…

Nick decided he needed a beer to cool off. He went to the small refrigerator behind the bar, asked his parents if they'd like one, and when they both shook their heads, he grabbed an extra for Chase, walking back to the pool table to hand it to him.

"Well, that's a fine how-do-you-do," Jessica complained. "Get your brother a beer and don't offer me one."

"You're the one who wanted to drive. That's the price you pay, Red. Besides, after riding with you, I don't even want to experience it after you've had alcohol."

"I'm a very good driver," she said. "We got here just fine, didn't we? And you're lucky I don't want to spoil the excellent taste of that pie with beer, or I'd be put out with you for trying to make my decisions for me."

"Whoa, big brother. I'd step back a pace if I were you," Chase teased.

"Naw. She doesn't scare me." Which was a bald-faced lie. She scared him right down to his toes. But he sure as hell didn't want *her* to know that.

He tugged at her curly red hair. "Better run the table while you have a chance, kiddo. Chase doesn't understand the concept of chivalry and letting girls win. He's too competitive."

Chase was the one who stepped back, because Jessica whirled around so fast she caught Nick off guard.

With a surprisingly strong finger, she poked him in the chest. "First off, I'm not a kiddo and I'm not a girl."

She inhaled, which expanded her chest, and his eyes naturally went that direction like a magnet drawn to the opposite pole. He really wanted to take a swig of beer, to cool his throat, but couldn't quite get his brain signals and motor skills in sync.

"Um, I beg to differ on that last part," he said, trying his best to take his eyes off her cleavage. She was much more generously endowed than the average woman.

"You got the gender right, pal, but you're way off the mark. Do you know how to spell *woman?*"

His eyes locked with hers and he didn't bother to answer the rhetorical question. She tapped a finger against her temple. "It's up here, pal. You might want to get a clue."

His brother made several taunting comments and his parents chuckled. Nick took a swig of beer, tried to act as though she hadn't just royally told him off.

Hell, he knew she was mature—both body and mind. But if he allowed himself to dwell on that too much, he could find himself in big trouble.

As it was, he was worried over the easy familiarity between Jessica and his brother. He'd never felt territorial like this, or...jealous, he realized.

Damn it. He wasn't jealous.

Never mind that Jessica and Chase were the same age, laughed easily, seemed perfectly suited for each other.

Chase wasn't the man for her.

And neither was Nick.

No matter how much his body wanted to deny it.

Chapter Six

After Jessica beat not only Chase at pool, but Nick and his father, too, they finally said their goodbyes and left.

"You forgot to mention you were a regular pool shark," Nick said as he slid into the fragrant new leather seats of the Tahoe.

She started the engine and put it in gear. Once again, she barely gave him time to buckle his seat belt.

Uh-oh, he thought. This was an entirely different woman from the one who'd been laughing and teasing inside the house moments ago.

Now that they didn't have to keep up appearances for his parents' sake, she'd gone silent again.

The headlights swung in an arc, catching the glowing eyes of a possum about to cross the driveway. Soon, the twin beams of the Tahoe were the only illumination along the road.

She drove fast, but he had to admit she did it competently. He shouldn't have been surprised.

Jessica was like a whirlwind, twirling him right into a vortex of confusion. Contradiction.

He was usually able to get a fairly accurate bead on his opponent—or his allies. Jessica Coleman defied his powers of deduction, kept him off balance.

He did know, though, that he hadn't been fair to her. And it was *his* problem, not hers.

"Look," he said, his voice sounding rough within the silent confines of the car. The radio was off and the air conditioner blew on high. "It's not easy for me to give up control. I've been running the company since Dad retired last year. Why don't we forget I gave you those two company files today, and we'll start fresh tomorrow."

She glanced at him and still managed to negotiate a hairpin turn with fairly impressive ease.

"Oh, no. I'm not forgetting a thing. Not until I've done all the research on those two businesses. You started this, Nick, and I'll see it through. In fact, I'm disappointed in you for backing down so soon."

"Man alive, I can't win for losing with you, can I?"

She shrugged. "Tell me one thing. Why have you held on to Striker and Jade Flyer when the reports I've seen so far indicate you should have dumped both companies six months ago?"

He leaned his head back against the leather headrest. "Both CEOs came to me when they were young and hungry. Both were long shots, but sometimes you make deals with friends or family of other business associates."

"And these two fall into that category."

"Yes." It was another lesson in not mixing business

and personal. "I hate to see people displaced. Closing a company or even selling it off will force people out of work."

"They'll be out of work, anyway, if the company goes bankrupt."

"I kept hoping something would turn around. I haven't had the time to figure out an option...hell, maybe I've been avoiding it."

They pulled into his circular driveway and Jessica shut off the engine, not making a move to get out. She turned to face him. The smell of her delicate floral perfume mingled with the new smell of leather. Her shoes were on the floorboard. With the night surrounding them, the hum of cicadas and crickets shut out by the insulated doors, it felt as though they were in a different world.

A world where he didn't feel like a mentor talking to a student. Jessica had a razor-sharp brain. He needed to give her credit for that.

"When I was in high school," he said, "a buddy of mine went through a bad patch when his father got laid off. I was surrounded by wealth, and though I wasn't in any way afraid of hard work—believed in it, actually—I was pretty well insulated from what my friend's family went through. They lost their house, had to move. Roger was on the verge of receiving a football scholarship. He changed, was embarrassed, you know?"

Nick raked a hand through his hair. "Watching the rug get jerked from beneath the feet of that proud family—through no fault of their own—made a lasting impact on me.''

''And you don't want the responsibility of doing that to anyone else. You'd rather absorb the loss yourself?''

''It's not just my decision to absorb the loss. The board's pressing for a solution or some kind of action. I just keep putting them off.''

''And now you're dumping it in my lap.''

''Yeah. And that was wrong. I'll meet with them tomorrow, come to terms.''

''Wait. Let me give it a try, Nick. I'm a fresh pair of eyes—and not personally involved like you are. Give me a chance to form my own impression, okay?''

''You think you can come up with something I missed?'' She kept catching him off guard with these subtle challenges. He wasn't used to it. His first instinct was to puff out his chest and tell her he knew best.

But something in the intelligence in her unique, dual-colored eyes kept him silent.

He didn't want to give up on Striker or Jade Flyer. Partly because it was personal, partly because it would affect so many lives, and partly because he hated to admit defeat. If Jessica had an idea, he owed it to everyone concerned to hear her out, give her the chance.

''Okay. I could use an unbiased opinion.''

She leaned over then, stunned him by pressing her soft lips to his. For the space of two heartbeats, he didn't react. Then his senses kicked in.

He jerked back, looked at her. Darkness surrounded

them. He'd just had a taste of the forbidden, a taste he'd longed for since the day he'd figured out that boys and girls were different.

Twelve years ago, he'd denied them both, knowing it was wrong for a man of twenty-one to have intimate feelings for a girl of thirteen. He'd turned his head and her innocent kiss had landed on his cheek.

This time, he wasn't going to turn his head, wasn't going to deny them.

Anticipation hung heavy in the humid air. Instead of letting her pull back, he gripped her shoulders, drew her forward until her breasts were resting against his chest and allowed himself to feast.

His mind went blank. He could only feel.

Resistance and surprise gave way to verve. She kissed him the way she did everything else in life. With her entire being. He didn't know what he'd been thinking, what he'd hoped to accomplish, but it hadn't been to get so swept away like this.

She invaded his senses. His heart pounded in his chest. Her lips were free of lipstick, so full and soft. Man alive, he could spend all night—the rest of his life—and be happy with just this.

Just this kiss.

The gentle pressure of her hands pushing against his chest brought him back to the moment. Hell. He'd been the one trying so damned hard to keep his distance, reminding himself this wasn't right, and then *she'd* had to be the one with enough sanity to call a halt.

She let out a breath, scooted back to her side of the truck. "That was..."

"My fault," he finished for her. "Damn, Jess. I'm sorry."

She stared at him, shook her head. "Do you know, you're the only man I've ever met who actually makes me have violent tendencies?" She reached for the door handle and let herself out of the car. "I swear I want to hit you more often than not."

Nick got out, too, and made his way to the front door, which was unlocked—just the way he'd left it. "Maybe if you *did* hit me I wouldn't do—"

She slapped a hand over his mouth. The urge to run his tongue along that smooth palm was overwhelming.

"Don't say another word," she cautioned. "It was just a kiss. No big deal. Criminy, you'd think this age thing was reversed and *you* were the younger one."

His brows slammed down. Her warning look kept his mouth shut. Damn it, this little spitfire confounded him.

"We've had a pleasant evening, so let's not spoil it with a fight. Deal?" She held out a hand for him to shake.

The gesture struck his funny bone. Especially after the heated kiss they'd just exchanged.

Feeling his lips twitch, he put his palm in hers. "Deal."

"Good. Now, do you mind if I act terribly civilized and use your pool?"

He lost the battle and grinned, remembering what

he'd said to her about swimming in the lake the other day.

"Be my guest. Or maybe I should say make yourself at home."

"Oh, I don't think I'll go that far. My parents have some silly idea that two weeks is a magical number for me to stay here. If you don't mind putting up with me, I'd like to humor them—ease their mind and hang around until then. In the meantime, I'll be looking for other arrangements."

"You can take as long as you need."

She laughed. "Said the man who just forced a coat hanger smile on his mouth. I imagine we can both manage to stay alive for two weeks."

"I imagine. Mind if I keep you company?"

"Where?" She'd lost the thread of the conversation somewhere.

"In the pool."

"Oh. Well." Hmmm. She couldn't very well say no. "It's your pool."

"If you want privacy, I'll give it to you."

She shrugged. "Suit yourself." Her heart rate went from fifty to a hundred in nothing flat. "I'll, uh, just go change into my suit."

Adrenaline singing through her veins, she ran up the stairs, terribly aware that Nick wasn't far behind her. So much for winding down the day in water. She should have kept her mouth shut and opted for the bathtub, instead.

On the other hand, the idea of Nick Grayson in swim trunks was too much of a curiosity to resist.

She just hoped to heaven it wasn't too much of a *temptation* to resist.

After that spontaneous kiss, she was feeling a mite off balance. Oh, sure, she'd started the whole thing. But it had been impulse. An instinctive kiss-it-and-make-it-better sort of thing.

Lord have mercy, it had turned into so much more.

Twelve years she'd waited to experience Nick Grayson's kiss. And then the darn man had apologized.

And, okay, he'd redeemed himself somewhat by talking *to* her in the car, rather than *at* her—given her a glimpse inside one of his deeper layers. But that didn't mean she should let down her guard.

Wishing she had a full-body wet suit, rather than the black bikini, she went downstairs, wrapped in an oversize towel.

Nick wasn't out there. Maybe he'd changed his mind. After all, she'd told him to suit himself, and he hadn't actually said whether or not he'd leave her to swim in private.

She dropped the towel on a chaise longue. Accent lighting illuminated the rockscape design of the pool and lush foliage that grew out of the crevices between boulders.

Water cascaded off rocks in a soothing waterfall. The subtle scent of chlorine and honeysuckle surrounded her as she eased down the steps, water enveloping her like liquid silk.

After the humidity of the day, it felt wonderful to relax and float and let the slightly heated water melt away the tension in her shoulders.

She gazed up at the stars, let out a breath. Movement caught the corner of her eye. A dark head appeared next to her shoulder.

She shrieked, sucked in a mouthful of pool water and sank like a rock.

Strong hands reached for her, pulled her up.

She coughed, could hardly draw in air. She felt masculine thighs beneath her hips, a palm smacking her on the back.

Nick had brought her over to the shallow end of the pool and sat on the steps, helpfully assisting her to get her breath back.

"Am I going to have to do mouth-to-mouth on you, Red?"

She coughed, shook her head, then slugged him on the shoulder.

"You scared the daylights out of me!"

"Ow," he complained, rubbing his shoulder. "That's the thanks I get for saving your life?"

"My life would have been perfectly serene if you hadn't sneaked up on me like that."

"I didn't sneak. I was here first."

"You were not. The pool was unoccupied. I checked."

"See that waterfall over there?"

"I have eyes."

"Well, you didn't use them very well. The edge of

the pool recesses in another two feet behind the waterfall. I was there the whole time.''

''Hiding.''

''Red?''

''What?''

With gentle fingertips, he smoothed back a strand of wet hair that clung to her cheek. ''Are you okay?''

She let out a breath. Her throat still felt scratchy and her voice had gone raspy like a two-pack-a-day smoker, but other than that, she was fine.

And she should not, she realized, be sitting on Nick Grayson's lap. Especially when his voice went all soft and caring like that.

She slid back into the water and put some distance between them.

''I'm fine, thank you for asking.'' She nearly laughed when his brows shot up, but refrained since she didn't want to swallow another gulp of pool water. Just to be ornery, she kicked her feet, splashing him in the face, then rolled over and began to swim.

She felt him grab her ankle and lost momentum, annoyed when he used her own body weight to propel himself past her.

''Cheater!'' Her competitive spirit raised, Jessica put all her strength into her forward stroke. They hit the waterfall at the same time. She somersaulted and used the side of the pool to shoot herself halfway back to the middle of the pool.

By the time she reached the shallow end again, Nick was a good five strokes behind her.

"See there," she said. "Cheating dogs never get fat."

He stood up and swept his hair back from his forehead. Water cascaded over his torso, and Jessica's tongue stuck to the roof of her mouth.

Oh...my...God. He was a dark-haired Adonis. Broad shoulders, tapered waist, just enough hair on his chest to make her bones dissolve in pure unadulterated lust.

"Why don't cheating dogs get fat?"

She thought about that for a moment, then shrugged. "I don't know. My mother says it."

He laughed, and the sound echoed on the honeysuckle-scented night air. "Then I guess it must be a fact. Did some competition swimming, hmm?"

"I considered trying out for the Olympics."

"I bet you'd have won the gold."

"Not with these boobs."

He was about to put his arms down, obviously satisfied that his hair was tidy enough. He froze for an instant, cleared his throat.

She laughed out loud. He was trying so darn hard not to look. Poor guy.

"Your..."

"Boobs," she repeated. "They were a handicap. Even though I tried to flatten them out beneath my suit, they definitely created a two-second time drag in the water that I never could break."

"Oh. Well...hmm."

His discomfort tickled her. It wasn't often that Nick

Grayson got flustered, and having been the one to cause it gave her great pride. ''Why, Nick, are you embarrassed?''

''Get real.'' He ducked down in the water and swam a few feet away.

Jessica stayed where she was on the steps in the shallow end.

When he reached the side of the pool, he put a hand on the edge to steady himself. She could barely see him. The yard lighting illuminated the grounds, but without the underwater flood turned on, the pool was as dark as river water.

Jessica shivered. She heard a splash, saw him go under the water and wondered what he was up to. She didn't like not knowing where he was. She wanted to keep the upper hand here.

And with Nick, that was an exhausting endeavor.

Straining her eyes toward the deep end and the waterfall, she jolted when he rose silently next to her.

''Nervous?'' he asked.

''Of course not.''

This time he did look at her chest. Blatantly. Appreciatively. ''It'd be a shame to have to hide those,'' he said softly.

She had a powerful urge to cross her arms. The black suit wasn't risqué by any means, but it did show quite a bit.

''I wasn't trying to hide them. Just get them out of the way.'' She ought to just shut up, because she was digging herself in deeper.

The sexy sparkle in his dark eyes was causing her nerve endings to hum. She didn't need to look down to see that her nipples were hard and clearly visible beneath the spandex suit.

Why did she feel so self-conscious all of a sudden? She'd never been particularly worried about swimming around men—heck, she'd grown up in a house full of men.

And though guys had ogled her body plenty of times, she'd gotten used to it, hardly ever noticed anymore. As a matter of fact, she rarely looked to see who was looking.

That was the thing about growing up around her three cowboy sheikh cousins. They possessed an innate confidence that had spilled over to her. And they'd never made her feel as though she couldn't do something because of her gender.

Alex, Cade and Mac had helped her see her worth as a person—and yes, a bit of their arrogance had rubbed off on her, as well. She wasn't a woman who needed to define herself through a man, was in no hurry to marry and do the domestic deal.

So it was perfectly silly to let her heart pound out of control like this, to wonder what Nick Grayson saw when he looked at her.

A woman or the young girl who'd made a fool out of herself years ago?

Did he see sexy curves or fat? The size of her breasts ensured that no one would ever call her a twig.

"Didn't your mama ever tell you it's not polite to stare, Red?"

She snapped out of her musings. By dog, she *was* staring at him. "Well, shoot. If you're gonna parade around half-naked, I'm bound to look."

Though her limbs were trembling, she was pretty proud of herself for carrying off the sophisticated bluff. Deciding to quit while she was ahead, she got out of the pool, casually picked up her towel and wrapped it around herself. "I think I'll call it a night."

He stayed in the water. She could hardly see him. "Night," he said softly.

She turned to go in, trying to walk with dignity and not trip. She could almost *feel* his eyes on her backside.

Lord have mercy, but the man was confusing the heck out of her. Why couldn't he just stay true to form and be his usual annoying self? Why did he have to be sexy…and fun…and…

"Forget it," she muttered, and let herself into the house through the sliding glass door. "I'm not extolling that man's virtues." About the time she did, he'd surely do his Jekyll and Hyde routine.

Nick stayed where he was and watched her go into the house. He didn't dare get out of the pool with the state his body was in. He'd tried so damned hard to steer clear of Jessica Coleman. But his body didn't seem to get the message his brain was signaling.

Man, he admired her spunk. She wasn't as self-assured as she wanted to appear, but he loved the way she never backed down.

She was a woman who would keep a man on his toes. He'd become weary lately of females who saw him as their ticket to wealth.

Now he'd run smack-dab up against a woman who could probably match him financially, and she was off-limits to him. A twenty-five-year partnership was at stake.

And he needed to remember that. He had no business toying with her, making intimate or suggestive remarks.

Hell, half the time, he didn't know which end was up around Jessica Coleman.

Chapter Seven

When Jessica left the house at six-thirty the next morning, the humidity was already on the rise. She pulled into the executive parking structure and noted that Nick's black Mercedes sedan was already there.

Darn it, did she have to get up in the middle of the night to beat him to the office? She always made sure she was early, and wanted the opportunity to gloat just a bit when he came in after her and passed by her office.

It seemed everything with her and Nick was a challenge, a rivalry. She wasn't sure how it had evolved that way over the years, but it was a trend that was very difficult to break. Or maybe a habit.

She flirted with the security guard in the lobby, then rode the elevator up to the seventh floor. The receptionist wasn't in yet, but the outer door was unlocked.

Obviously by Nick.

Rather than seeking him out, she went directly to her corner office and brewed a pot of coffee, gazing out the window for a few minutes, enjoying the dawning of a new day. The Dallas skyline was beautiful this morning, the buildings and fine architecture crowded together in all shapes and sizes like proud natives anxious to tell their history. Smog hadn't yet gathered as the world was just coming alive.

When the coffeepot beeped, she poured herself a cup, added cream and sugar, then sat down at her desk to review the folders she'd begun to investigate yesterday.

The companies Nick had given her to evaluate weren't their usual type of acquisition. Coleman-Grayson invested mostly in Dow Jones and Nasdaq companies. But they did provide start-up funds for several local Texas firms—like Striker and Jade Flyer—that appeared to have solid potential for growth.

The company slogan stenciled on the light-gray walls of the reception area said, "Coleman-Grayson, the people who invest in people and the community."

Well, Jessica intended to get a firsthand look at one of the "people" projects that appeared to be floundering.

She used the early morning to catch up on the *Wall Street Journal* and check the latest stock prices over the Internet. As employees came to work, the phone lines lit up, and the hum of business being conducted filled the air.

Placing a phone call to Jade Flyer's CEO, she set up a meeting for 10:00 a.m. and made some last-minute notes.

After slipping into her summer-weight, olive-tone

suit jacket, she grabbed her stack of reports and made her way out of the office.

Reading and walking at the same time, she nearly had a heart attack when she ran into a solid wall of human flesh.

"Oh, my gosh. I'm so sor—" For no good reason, other than it was Nick Grayson she'd slammed into, her apology dried up.

He reached out to steady her. "Are you okay?"

Darn it, he *would* have to be nice. Even though he'd offered to take the projects back and start over, she had enough leftover pique to have her stomach clench when she saw him, to have her I'll-show-you antenna still vibrating.

They both bent at the same time to pick up the scattered contents of the folder that had been knocked out of her hands.

"I'm fine." When they latched on to the same piece of paper and appeared destined to a game of tug-of-war, Jessica sighed and gave a soft laugh. "Seems like we're bound to clash, no matter what."

He stared at her for a long moment, his gaze mapping her face, her hair, her body. She had no idea what was going through his mind, but the intensity of his look was almost a tangible caress.

Mesmerized, she went absolutely still, had trouble drawing a breath. What in the world?

A telephone ringing in the next office broke the spell. "Where were you headed?" he asked.

"I've got a meeting with Brandon Frenchie over at Jade Flyer." They both stood.

"You work fast. Mind if I go with you?"

"What, you don't trust me to do this on my own?"

He sighed. "I guess I deserved that. It's not that I don't trust you, Jess. It's that you've made me see I can't put off concerns that need immediate action or base business decisions on emotions or friendships."

"I forgot. You and Brandon are friends, aren't you."

"In a way. I went to school with his brother."

She motioned for him to follow if he wanted, then stopped by the reception desk and told Anna where she'd be.

"Same here, Anna," Nick said. "Tell Rhonda to get me on the cell if she needs anything."

"Cell phones." Jessica punched the button in the hallway to call the elevator. "Where would we be without them?"

"Probably a lot freer and less stressed. Especially when certain people don't answer theirs."

She grinned and brushed her hair back behind her shoulders. She should have worn it up this morning, but decided she wanted to go for a younger look for the meeting. Through her research she'd learned that the staff at Jade Flyer were predominately young and unconventional.

"They invented caller ID for a reason, Grayson. Besides, I saved myself a quarter on an unnecessary incoming call."

The elevator arrived and they rode it down to the

parking level. ''Unnecessary,'' he repeated, holding the doors as she exited. ''We probably ought to get it straight right now that I don't make calls that aren't important.''

She raised her brows, inviting him to debate what had been so ''important'' about his checking her whereabouts.

He wisely dropped the subject, but touched her arm, indicating she was going the wrong way. ''My car's over there.''

''And mine's right in front of us.'' Sure enough, the red Tahoe was ten feet away. ''We're not going to go through this old song again, are we? It's my meeting. I imagine I can get us there.''

''When did you get so damned independent?''

''I've always been independent. You've just made such a point of avoiding me, you haven't noticed.''

This time it was his brows that lifted. ''All right,'' she conceded. ''I understand why you backed off when I was young. That still doesn't excuse being unobservant during the ensuing years.''

He got in her car when she unlocked the door, quickly buckling his seat belt. ''In case you've forgotten, we haven't exactly been on great terms in those ensuing years.''

''True. If you hadn't been so priggish, maybe things would have been different.''

''Priggish? You admitted just last night that you understood. That you were too young.''

"Or you were too old," she countered, biting her lower lip when his brows drew together.

"Whatever. By your own admission you hated me. You have to take some responsibility here, admit that your attitude didn't foster friendly relations."

"I'm sure I'd have been more than willing to compromise if you hadn't turned everything into an order every time we spoke on the phone."

She pulled out of the parking garage and into the morning downtown-Dallas traffic. Surreptitiously she glanced at the map by her thigh.

"Turn right at the signal, then left on Commerce."

"I have the directions."

"Just trying to be helpful."

"Thank you. But this is my show today." She stopped at a red light. "I want your promise right now that you won't try to take over. You either give me your word you'll keep quiet and let me handle this my way, or I'll take you back to the office."

A horn honked behind her.

The light had changed, but Jessica didn't take her foot off the brake.

Nick glanced in the side-view mirror. "You're holding up traffic."

"Your word," she repeated.

"Fine, you have my word."

That was the one thing she did trust about Nick Grayson. His word. She wiggled her fingers in an apologetic gesture to the car behind her and made the turn.

The impatient motorist followed her, then sped

around to pass. Jessica knew the guy was irritated. She looked to her left and gave him a dazzling smile, lowered the window and called, ''Sorry, sugar. Daydreaming. What can I say?''

He returned her smile and gave a friendly wave that seemed to say, ''No problem.''

''How many tickets have you charmed your way out of with that flirty act?'' Nick asked.

''Not a single one. I've never been pulled over by the police.''

''You can probably kiss that record goodbye.''

''Why?''

''The way you drive?'' His tone suggested he couldn't believe she'd even asked the question. ''That and this red paint job. You're a siren magnet.''

''Is that why you drive a black car? So you'll blend in?''

''If I wanted to blend in, I'd probably choose white.''

''True.'' They were actually conversing in a somewhat civil manner now. Oh, they had their moments—like during that kiss last night.

They weren't *always* at each other's throats.

Just most of the time.

Without further directions from Nick, she pulled into the parking lot of Jade Flyer. It was a trendy shop attached to a good-size warehouse where they designed and built specialty skateboards.

Getting out of the car, she put her jacket back on—

she'd removed it for the drive—and waited for Nick to fall into step beside her.

"Can I at least speak long enough to introduce you?" Nick asked.

She laughed. "If it's necessary, yes. But I'm telling you, I don't have too many shy bones in this body. I can hold my own."

They went in through the back warehouse door. It could have been a weekend—the company barely had a skeleton crew working. The smell of plastic, lubricating oil and acrylic paint hung in the air.

"That's Frenchie over there," Nick said, nodding to a young man with long blond hair pulled back in a ponytail and a T-shirt with the Jade Flyer logo on the front and back.

"Hey, dude," Brandon called. Without warning, the guy sent a skateboard scooting across the room.

Nick stopped it with his foot, then pushed off and rode it across the concrete floor of the warehouse.

Jessica was impressed. His Italian loafers weren't the greatest for gripping the board, and he jumped off at the last minute, leaving Brandon to catch the runaway skateboard.

"Not bad, man. You still got it."

"Still?" Jessica asked, joining them. She stuck out her hand. "I'm Jessica Coleman."

"Glad to meet you. Brandon Frenchie. And didn't Nick tell you? He not only sponsored a couple of our competitions, man, he competed on our team, too."

Hmm. Wasn't that interesting? She couldn't imagine

Nick in a pair of baggie shorts and T-shirt maneuvering a skateboard over a horseshoe-shaped ramp, being judged on turns and the height of jumps.

Frankly, just watching the competitions scared the very devil out of her. Major testosterone going on. Scary stuff.

And straitlaced Nick? Well, well.

"Hey, cool," Brandon said, peering into her eyes. "You wearing two different-color contact lenses?"

"Nope. Fluke of nature."

"Radical."

Nick tugged at his suit-coat sleeves and watched as Jessica smoothly engaged Brandon in conversation, expressing interest and putting the young CEO at ease in a matter of seconds.

Never mind that Brandon practically had to pick his tongue up off the floor when he got a good look at Jessica's figure. *He* certainly couldn't have gotten away with such a blatant show of stunned appreciation, Nick thought.

Innate sensuality wafted off her like the subtle floral scent of her perfume, as much a part of her as her Texas accent. She was clearly aware of her effect on men, but she didn't make an issue of it.

And because she didn't, it made a man take a step back, feel ashamed of himself. Then, in a move so smooth most would miss it, she drew in her captive audience with verve, enthusiasm and genuine intelligence.

She gave her complete attention to Brandon, listened

intently to every word he said, yet at the same time, Nick didn't think she missed a single bit of her surroundings.

"I've gone over your finances, Brandon. You've got sponsorship, low overhead, and your debt ratio isn't too far out of line."

"Until the last six months, you mean. Hey, I know we're in a mess. The competition caught up with us. We figured our name was big enough to carry us. Guess that's what we get for overconfidence, huh?"

"I think you've just suffered a bad patch and gotten a bit overwhelmed. You've got too many of your eggs in one basket."

"Dude, we're a skateboard company. We only had one basket to start with, and it was riding high for a lot of years."

"But it's about to crash and burn now, isn't it?"

She didn't appear offended that Brandon had called her *dude*. In some circles, it was a unisex word. It still caught Nick off guard. He figured if a guy was going to be in business, he ought to take care to use a more conservative vocabulary.

"Yeah. We're losing money every day we pay our employees to come to work when we barely have enough orders to cover the utilities. And I know you've got a stake in this, too. We don't blame you for being worried about the investment."

"So do something about it."

"What? I've quit drawing a paycheck, and so has Sean, my main man."

''Sean Tilden. Jade Flyer's vice president.''

''Yeah, that's him.''

She stopped and looked around the vast warehouse with its various machines. ''No sense being in business if it's not making you a living. Why don't you reorganize your workforce, do something different? You went into this business because skateboards were in such high demand. Why don't you manufacture something else, as well—like scooters? They're the hot ticket right now.''

''You know how many companies are doing scooters?''

''Probably about the same number that are doing skateboards.'' She paused to let her point sink in. ''Don't shy away from competition, Brandon. Join it. Do some advertising, trade on your Jade Flyer name in the industry.''

She went over to a workstation, trailed her fingers through a bin filled with silver ball bearings. ''You've already got the wheels and the equipment. It's just a matter of retooling some, making adjustments. It's feasible.''

''Maybe...''

''Come out with a new color,'' she said. ''A flashy paint job bearing the Jade Flyer logo. Do some sort of reflective lights inside the wheels—or outside them.''

Brandon nodded enthusiastically. ''Neon. Strobes. Black lights.''

''There you go. Make some contacts in the field. Find out how much it would cost to motorize them, even. Offer both—standard and the motorized versions. Beef up your Web site. Start taking preorders."

Brandon whooped and picked Jessica up, twirling her around. She laughed and grabbed his shoulders. When he set her down, he planted an enthusiastic kiss on her smiling lips.

Nick clenched his fists. He'd given his word not to interfere in the business dealings. There'd been no mention of not stepping in if the customer started mauling the investor.

"You're totally rad, Jessica. Why didn't I think of this before?"

"Probably because you were too close to it."

"Kind of like lookin' at the waves and not seeing the whole ocean? Man, you're a smart lady—I mean it."

At least he hadn't said smart *for* a lady. That might have goosed her red-haired temper. Brandon was genuinely complimenting her.

Nick relaxed, since there wasn't any more lip locking going on. In all honesty, he was damned impressed himself. Watching her in action, he realized she had a gift for looking at something and knowing what would work.

The intriguing part was that she didn't appear to realize she had the special talent. Her clever brain took an idea and simply ran with it.

And it made perfect sense. She did it on the wing. Spontaneous.

Something Nick rarely did.

From then on, he followed her with a different attitude.

Before the morning was over, he was both awed and confused by what appeared to be scatterbrained logic. She dazzled every one of the employees with her smile, yet held their attention and respect with her suggestions.

Excitement crackled like electricity in the air. Hell, she'd even snagged a janitor when they realized they didn't have enough board members for a quorum, and ignoring the parliamentary procedures outlined in Robert's Rules of Order, she'd spearheaded an impromptu election so Brandon and Sean could put the wheels in motion immediately.

By the time all was said and done and they were in her car headed back to the office, Nick felt as if he'd been led on a wild escapade where there were no rules and the pace was so vigorous he had trouble catching his breath.

"Well?" she asked as they made their way back to downtown Dallas. "You've gone awfully quiet."

"You told me not to butt in."

She glanced at him and he realized she was nervous. She wanted validation or approval of her decisions.

He'd expected her to gloat. Not seek his opinion.

"You were pretty amazing back there."

She let out a breath. "Do you think it's a viable plan?"

"Yes. And the kids at that company have the enthusiasm to make it work." Kids, he thought. Brandon was probably around Jessica's age, maybe a little older. When had he started feeling older than everyone else?

Sure, he'd been responsible from a young age, but that was no excuse to become staid.

Jessica had called him stuffy. And priggish. He didn't like the thought that the metaphorical shoe fit so well.

This was the magic of his dad's and Randy Coleman's partnership, he realized. Jared Grayson and Randy Coleman had been two entirely different individuals, yet complemented each other's personality. Jared had connections and Randy had innovative ideas.

Much the same as Jessica and him.

He wished he didn't feel threatened by her head for business.

Was that his problem?

Or was it more personal, wanting something he shouldn't—couldn't—allow himself to have?

THE OUTING with Jessica to Jade Flyer put Nick behind schedule. He made it to a lunch meeting, but phone calls and obligations had backed up on him.

It was five o'clock before he walked back into the office, and he still had a mountain of work waiting for him on his desk.

For some reason, his concentration and powers of organization were off today.

Walking by Jessica's office, he was drawn by her laughter. He didn't mean to pause by the doorway and eavesdrop on her conversation, but when he heard her mention his brother's name, human nature had him tuning in.

Just knowing the sound of her laughter was directed at another man made his gut clench.

That it was toward his own brother made it worse. What was Chase thinking? It was so easy to get drawn in by Jessica's verve and spontaneity.

Nick knew he had no right to dictate her social life, but, damn it, his brother was a playboy, definitely not a sticking-around kind of guy. And that's what Jessica needed. Someone who was willing and able to commit.

Before he even realized he was going to do it, he knocked on her open office door. "Can I interrupt for a minute?"

She paused, held up a finger. "Hold on a sec, Chase." Then she pressed the hold button on the receiver and looked expectantly at him. "Did you need something?"

"Yeah. I overheard you making dinner plans, but I need you to work late tonight."

Without waiting for her to accept or decline, he walked away. He told himself he was protecting her, and not acting out of jealousy.

He'd never had occasion to feel jealous of his brother, had a great relationship with him.

But this was different. The past often dictated the future. And if Chase had a tendency to forget that, then Nick would have to be the responsible one and remind him.

He was in his office when she stormed in.

"Where do you get off demanding overtime and not even waiting to see if the other party is agreeable?"

"You're the one who wanted more responsibility. Have you changed your mind?"

Jessica had a fierce urge to take off one of her low-heeled pumps and chuck it at him. He could be so smug sitting there behind that desk. "No, I haven't changed my mind. What's so urgent it can't wait till morning?"

"Lusklow. Since the meeting's been postponed, it gives me an opportunity to scrutinize the financial records, look for discrepancies we might otherwise miss if we were rushed for time."

Jessica sighed. The mention of Lusklow reminded her of the man's ill wife. Some of the wind blew out of her sail.

"Do you at least plan to eat?" she asked.

"I asked Rhonda to have sandwiches delivered from the deli."

"For me, too?"

"Yes."

"Awfully sure of yourself, aren't you?"

"Not of myself. Of you."

"Well. A compliment. We're making progress." She kicked off her shoes and put her hands on her hips. "Okay, where do you want me to start?"

He gazed at her bare feet for several moments.

"What?" she asked. "We have to stay appropriately attired after hours? I don't know about you, but that's practically against my principles."

His gaze returned to her face. "Take off whatever you like."

"Now there's a suggestion I could scare you to death with." She didn't think he'd meant his words as innuendo. "What do you want me to do?"

Flustered, he ran a hand through his hair, but was saved answering when Rhonda knocked on the door and brought in their dinner.

"The deli sent this up," the secretary said. "If you don't need me for anything else, I'll be heading home."

"Thanks, Rhonda. Go ahead."

"You don't work too late now, boss. You hear?"

He smiled, and Jessica felt a pang of annoyance. Why was it so easy for him to smile and speak sweetly to everyone except her?

"I hear, Rhonda. Thanks for your help today."

"It's my job."

It was more than that. Rhonda loved her work. And it showed. Come to think of it, Jessica realized that the staff at Coleman-Grayson was a highly motivated, dedicated, upbeat group of individuals. There wasn't a lot of back stabbing and malicious gossip going on in the office. People were professional, friendly and helpful.

Had that been Nick's father's training? Or had Nick had a hand in shaping the attitudes, too?

Jessica went to the small refrigerator in the corner of the office and perused the contents. Sodas, bottled water and a nice chablis.

"Do you have rules about having wine with dinner at the office?"

"My life isn't totally governed by rules, Jess."

She shrugged. Her mother had always told her actions spoke louder than words. And according to Nick's actions, he indeed *was* a man governed by rules.

Rules imposed on himself. Rules to succeed, to live by, to work by—to be intimate by.

Oh, no. She wasn't even going to go there.

She took the white wine out of the fridge, along with two bottles of water.

"Do you want a glass?" she asked.

"Unless you have in mind passing the wine bottle back and forth, it'd probably be a good idea."

She retrieved two crystal glasses out of the cabinet. "Actually, some friends and I went to a party where we did that."

His dark brows lifted. "What kind of party was that?"

She laughed. "A college, see-how-drunk-we-can-get party."

"I went to a couple of those," he said. "But we stuck to our own bottles or glasses."

"Smart of you. I ended up with strep throat and missed two weeks of classes." She set her sandwich on the coffee table by the leather sofa in the sitting area of his office, then poured them each a glass of wine and took his over to his desk.

His sleeves were rolled up to the elbows, his tie loosened at the neck, the top collar of his shirt unbuttoned.

Each time she took an unguarded opportunity to really look at him, she was struck by the handsome masculinity of his features. He was the kind of man that made women turn on the streets and stare, or do stupid things like walk into a post or trip over a curb.

Of course those infatuation days were behind her, Jessica assured herself. Now if her knees wouldn't tremble at the sight of him, she might be able to convince herself it was the truth.

Chapter Eight

"So, what's on the agenda?" she asked, waving a hand at the papers on Nick's desk.

He gathered up several three-ring binders and pushed them toward her. "I've got Lusklow's financial records for the past five years. I've gone over the oldest records and have been moving forward. Why don't you take the current year and last year?"

"Okeydoke. What am I looking for?"

"The big picture. Inconsistencies. Anything that raises a red flag that might not get mentioned until after a deal closes."

Jessica knew her way around financial statements and bookkeeping. Lusklow had a solid reputation in the software industry, but with investments that reached into the millions, it wasn't smart to leave anything to chance.

She ate half of her sandwich, then curled her feet under her on the sofa and got comfortable. The buildings that formed the Dallas skyline beyond the office windows began to twinkle with electric lighting as day melted into night.

Most people would be home with their families or out for dinner or settled in to watch their favorite television program by now.

If her apartment had still been intact, Jessica probably would have grabbed a frozen dinner, taken a dip in the pool, then piled up in bed poring over maps and financial analysis of a special project she'd been gathering information on recently.

Actually, she'd have had a fun dinner with Chase, and *then* perched in the middle of the bed to work.

The idea she'd been working on excited her, but she needed to take things slow. She wanted to have all her guns loaded before she made a presentation to Nick and the other stockholders.

Absorbed in the reports before her, her mind automatically calculating debt ratios and past product performance, she looked up when the sound of soft rock music filled the office.

Nick brought the bottle of wine over to the couch and rubbed the back of his neck. "I'm getting a crick. What do you say we take a break for a minute?"

"Sure."

He topped off the wine in her glass and sat down on the sofa, leaving an entire cushion between them.

Without thought, Jessica scooted up on her knees and reached over to knead his shoulders.

He stiffened.

"Would you relax?" She tugged until he shifted forward, giving her access to his tense muscles.

For a moment the room spun, and she automatically looked at the level of wine in her glass. She'd only eaten half her sandwich, but she'd had two glasses of wine.

"You have nice hands," he murmured, letting his head drop forward.

"Of course I do." And the feel of his skin beneath her palms was having a direct effect on her breathing. On her knees, her thigh was touching his arm, and every time she kneaded, her breasts came within a whisper of his back.

She wanted, suddenly, in the worst way to lean forward and let them press. To feel the solid wall of his body against that sensitive part of hers.

To revel in their masculine and feminine differences.

And if she didn't detour her thoughts, she was going to be drooling down his neck.

"Do you always work so much?" she asked. The gold clock on his desk ticked loudly in the quiet office. They were the only two left in the building, she suspected, noting that it was nearly ten o'clock.

"Do you object to putting in overtime? Because if you do, then maybe you're not right—"

"I don't object." She took a breath, counted to ten, squeezed a little harder at the base of his neck. "But I have a life outside of work. I enjoy getting together with friends."

"My brother?"

This time she counted to twenty. ''As a matter of fact, yes.''

He sat up straight and her hands fell away from his shoulders. ''That's not a good idea.''

''Are you jealous?''

''Get real.''

''Then what's the big deal?''

''Chase isn't right for you.''

She wanted to shake him. Or smack him. Emotions burst to the surface, faster than she could process.

''And I suppose you're going to tell me who *is* right for me.'' She had to get off this couch, away from him. ''I swear, you are the most arrogant, pigheaded, bossiest, fuddy-duddy I've ever—''

She shrieked when he grabbed her wrists to stop her from getting up, toppling her into his lap, instead.

His expression was fierce. Both of them were breathing hard, as though they'd been physically wrestling, instead of just snapping heated words.

She became aware of the fire in his eyes, the hard ridge of desire she could feel beneath her thighs.

Anger gave way to confusion.

How could she be so annoyed with him one moment, then want to devour him the next? And why did that little lick of fear deep in her belly excite her?

She thought she knew what desire felt like. She realized she'd had no earthly idea.

Her heart bumped against her chest. The passionate emotions inside her needed an outlet.

"Damn it," he murmured. "I'm tired of fighting this. I don't think I *can* fight it anymore."

His head lowered and his lips fused with hers. It wasn't an easy kiss, the kind that began as persuasion and ended in passion. This kiss started in full-blown passion.

If there had been steps one and two, he bypassed them and went straight to three.

His palm slid up her thigh, beneath her skirt and cupped her behind, pulling her into him in a way that left little doubt what was on his mind.

She wrapped her arms around his neck, dove into the kiss, seeking something, but she wasn't sure what it was.

This was new territory. Yet it felt like coming home. She'd dreamed of being in his arms so often that it seemed as though she'd been there all her life.

He raised his head and she whimpered.

"Don't stop. Please..." If he did what he'd done to her twelve years ago, she didn't think she'd recover.

"I can't stop," he said, his voice sandpaper rough.

In a frenzy of mouths clinging and bodies straining, he managed to get her top off. She tugged at his tie, popped a button on his shirt and jerked it off his shoulders. Her skirt was up around her waist like a sash. When he released the back hook of her bra, her breasts spilled forward, at last brushing the naked skin of his chest.

Oh, it was so much better than imagination. Warm. Soft against hard. Lying partially on her side across lap, her left breast rested against the right, the plump swell of both reaching nearly to her throat.

He ran his fingertips over the indentation on her shoulder left by her bra strap, then cupped his palm beneath the heavy weight of her breast. The feel of his hand, so gentle, kneading, lifting, stroking, nearly sent her over the edge.

For once she didn't feel as if her breasts were the object of a man's lust, but actually cherished.

And for once, she truly felt sexy, instead of faking it.

His lips lowered to her nipple. She raised up to give him better access, straining against him. Desire pulled like a taut string from her chest to her thighs. The feeling was exquisite, so new, so exciting.

A little fearful, yes. She wasn't sure what to expect.

She only knew that she'd waited way too long.

And this was a journey she wanted to take.

With Nick.

Unable to keep her hands still, she ran her palms over his shoulders, his back, up his chest and into his hair, pulling his head more firmly into the cushioned valley of her breasts.

He moaned, worshiped her incredibly sensitive skin with his lips and tongue, then slid his hand down and cupped her through her panties.

Jessica nearly fainted. The pleasure was so intense she actually held her breath until she saw stars. Then enormous emotions welled up inside her. She wanted to beg, but wasn't sure what to beg for.

Her hands and body became a frantic mass of nerves. She strained and stretched and rubbed against him, pressing, pushing…hurrying.

"Wait," he said when her hand stroked down his abdomen, beneath the zipper of his trousers, grazing the moist tip of him.

"No." Her breath was coming in pants now. "I don't want to wait. I need…" She didn't know what she needed, didn't know the words to tell him.

"I know what you need," he murmured as though reading her thoughts.

He kicked off his pants, shifted her beneath him on the couch. "Put your legs around me."

She did as he asked. He'd removed her panties and now all she wore was the skirt bunched around her waist like a silky belt.

Her breasts flattened beneath his subtle weight. He held himself off her, but applied just enough erotic pressure to have her digging her heels into his calves, scraping her nails against his buttocks, urging him to complete this journey of discovery.

So long. She'd waited so long.

She felt the tip of him against her like velvety hot steel.

"Nick!" She bucked her hips and at the same time he pushed forward.

Her scream of pleasure hitched. But only for the barest of seconds. And then she was flying. She couldn't catch her breath, yet at the same time felt as if she was hyperventilating.

He eased in and out of her, faster, harder, higher. With his hands beneath her bottom, he cupped her, lifted her, angled her in a way that caused his thrusts to ignite a storm of sensation she'd never before experienced, sensations that defied description.

She could only feel, ride the waves, marvel at the wild, wonderful spasms racking her body. Her breasts were slick where they chaffed against his chest. Her fingertips slipped off his shoulders, dug into his back.

She couldn't take a second more. It was too much. The pleasure too intense. And oh, she wanted it to go on for a lifetime. She rode the crest of an incendiary climax, reveled in it, felt him throb inside her, heard him call her name.

She might have actually fainted, after all. She didn't know. Her body had just experienced something phenomenal.

She felt his heart thundering against hers. "Jess?"

"Shh." She wrapped her arms around his back, held him still with the strength of her legs twining with his. She was dizzy—with desire or fatigue, she wasn't sure. She was afraid if either of them spoke, it would break the spell. Just a few minutes more, she thought. A few minutes more of bliss before either of them could formulate regrets.

She felt him relax against her, ease into sleep.

Minutes turned into hours. She stroked his back, unable to shut her own eyes. What had she done?

She'd slept with the enemy, that was what. At least,

the man she'd told herself for the past twelve years was the enemy.

And if she continued to lie here like this, feel the press of his warm body against hers, she would start building castles in the air around him, just as she'd done when she was a girl.

How unsophisticated could she be? The man probably had dozens of one-night stands under his belt, and what had transpired between them would be no big deal for him.

The last thing she should do was let him know it had been a big deal to her.

As quietly as possible, she inched out from beneath him and scooped up her clothes. It was nearly four o'clock in the morning.

She had some plans to make, some decisions.

NICK COULDN'T BELIEVE he'd fallen asleep. The sun wasn't yet up, but the sky wasn't pitch-dark like it had been when he'd closed his eyes five hours before.

He was sprawled naked on the office sofa.

Alone.

His heart pumped in his chest. Was it all a dream? He sat up, grabbed for his suit pants, looked toward the bathroom.

The room was dark. Jessica's clothes were gone. The only sign that she'd even been here was the half-eaten sandwich on the coffee table and a second crystal glass next to his with a smudge of coral lipstick on the rim.

And the memory of her incredibly soft body beneath him, the passion she'd given so freely and vocally.

The word that flashed in his mind was *real.* There had been no coyness about her, nothing tidy or quiet about her emotions. Without hesitation, without restraint, she'd opened herself to him.

How the hell had he fallen asleep? How had she left without waking him?

And *why* had she left without waking him?

She'd been a virgin. Who would have known? The woman had a body that wouldn't quit and talked and sassed like she had plenty of experience.

She'd *acted* as though she had plenty of experience.

He remembered the frenzy of her hands, the straining of her body. She hadn't been shy, hadn't given him a hint that this was her first time.

Damn it, they were residing under the same roof, a perfectly fine home that had plenty of beds and ambiance. And Jessica was a woman who deserved ambiance.

Yet her first time had been on a leather sofa in his office.

"Great going, Grayson." He ought to be shot.

In another three hours, he'd need to be back in this office. But first he had to find Jessica, make sure she was all right, apologize and find out how much damage had been done to their ability to work together.

He swore as he raced out of the empty parking garage and onto the eerily quiet streets of downtown Dallas.

The interior of the Mercedes smelled like leather, but he could have sworn he detected the fragrance of flowers somewhere nearby. And sex.

He licked his lips, took his hand off the steering wheel and lifted it to his nose. The scent, he realized, was coming from him.

The scent of Jessica.

His body reacted like a randy teenager's. He rolled down the window, breathed in the familiar smell of peach orchards and rich earth. He had to get himself under control.

In his mind, he rehearsed his apology, his logical explanation of passion overcoming reason. *It happens,* he told himself.

It didn't mean it had to *continue* to happen. They could be adults about this.

He'd have to make her see what was at stake. Surely she'd agree with him that they should each retreat to their respective corners and regroup.

The headlights arced across the white fences and verdant lawns as he turned into his driveway. Jessica's Red Tahoe was under the porte-cochere.

She was probably in bed.

God, he hadn't felt so unsure of himself since he was a kid waiting to see if he'd made the Little League team.

If she was asleep, he'd leave her be, wait until morning and see how she acted toward him. Maybe he wasn't giving her enough credit. She wasn't a little girl.

She could handle the emotions of a man and woman getting carried away by passion.

Yeah, right. Like she's done this sort of thing before.

He swore. It had been up to him to protect her, to be the one with the backbone. He'd blown it. And now he had to fix it. Gently. Without harming her feelings or causing a rift that would rip apart the business.

The lights were on in her bedroom. He mounted the stairs, his heart pounding.

She was taking her clothes out of the closet, laying them across the bed.

Packing.

His gut twisted as though someone had reached a fist inside him and yanked.

"Thanks for leaving me in the buff for my secretary to find." That hadn't been what he'd meant to say.

She jolted, paused, then took another skirt off the hanger. "I locked your office door. You were safe."

Yeah, he'd nearly torn the knob off, expecting it to turn easily. "What are you doing?" *Perfect, Grayson. You're doing just perfect.*

"Since I don't think you've gone blind in the last few hours, I imagine you can see for yourself. This just isn't going to work, Nick. It's for the best."

Never mind that was exactly what he'd planned to say, hearing the words come from her sent his emotions into a panic. He didn't understand it.

He only knew that he didn't want her to go yet. Regardless of his rehearsed speech to the contrary. It would be like running away, leaving a project undone.

They needed to explore what had happened between them, prove that they could remain on an even keel, give him time to analyze it the way he usually did with something that puzzled him.

For twelve years, ever since that incident with the kiss, he'd held himself under tight control around Jessica for fear of taking her innocence.

And now he'd done what he'd fought so hard not to do.

And damn, even knowing it was wrong, the sight of her, the smell of her, the remembered feel of her, wouldn't go away.

He wanted more.

Jessica folded a stack of underwear she'd taken out of the dresser and absently stroked the silk.

Her breath backed up in her lungs when she sensed the heat of Nick's body just behind hers, felt the touch of his hand as he placed it over the top of hers, stilling her motions.

She made a fist, scrunching the silk panties in her grip. He didn't let go.

"Why didn't you tell me?"

Oh. She wished a hole would suddenly open in the floor and swallow her. She knew what he was asking. Embarrassment heated her cheeks.

She slipped her hand from beneath his and stepped away. "I guess I was a little preoccupied." She tried to sound flip. He obviously wasn't having any of it.

"I could have hurt you."

"Criminy, Nick, do you talk the act to death with all your lovers?"

He took her arm, turned her to face him. "You're not *all* my lovers, Jess. You're a family friend, a partner in our business. I promised your father I'd take care of you, not take advantage."

"Oh, stop it. Nobody takes advantage of me." She glared at him. "No one. I was as much a party to what went on between us as you were."

"But I'm the one with the experience."

"You say that as though it makes you better than me. More worldly—"

"Damn it, Jess—"

"Don't you swear at me."

He raked a hand through his hair. "Can't we have a conversation without one or both of us shouting?"

She shrugged. "Evidently not. Which is another reason I'm removing myself from your home." She turned back to the closet. "We both need privacy."

"Don't go."

The very softness of his voice stopped her, deflated her agitation quicker than a pin stuck in a balloon. Slowly she let go of the hanger she'd been about to remove, and turned to face him.

"Nick—"

"Hear me out. It's a big house, Jess."

"So you think that'll change anything?"

"If we shift our goal, it will. You came here to learn the ins and outs of the business. I'll start bringing files home at night. Give me one month. You can pick my brain, go where I go, see who I see. Twenty-four-seven, you'll have my undivided attention—solely focused on business.''

He was handing her exactly what she'd wanted—what she'd come here for. A little late, perhaps.

She searched for signs that he was pitying her after what had happened between them on the office sofa.

But his dark eyes were serious.

''Why now?'' She had to ask it.

''Because I've been a jerk.''

Her brows raised. He wasn't going to get an argument there.

''Look, I've spent a lot of years fighting an attraction for you, an obsession, I guess,'' he admitted. ''So I thought I'd keep my distance, stay away from the office and temptation. Stay away from you. I'm a guy, Jess...'' His words trailed off as though he couldn't find the right ones to explain himself.

''So, now that you've given in to temptation, satisfied the curiosity, you think you can get it out of your system?''

''Can you?''

She could have clobbered him for turning the question around on her. If she said no, it'd put them right back where they'd been twelve years ago—leaving herself wide open for rejection.

If she said yes, she'd be lying. Nick Grayson had been in her system all her life. It would take more than a night in his arms to change that.

She sat down on the bed, feeling more vulnerable than she liked.

"Is it me, Nick?" Was she still too young? Too fat? Too pushy? Too…whatever?

He shook his head. "It's not you. It's *us*. It's who we are." He leaned against the dresser. "Do you remember Chase's engagement to Laura Timms?"

"No."

"Laura was the daughter of my mom's best friend, Eve. To make a long story short, Chase and Laura had a nasty breakup and it ended up ruining Mom and Eve's friendship. It was pretty devastating for all of us."

"What does that have to do with me?"

"Don't you see? You and I have even more to lose. Both our families do. Just because we burned up the sheets together—"

"The couch," she corrected.

"Yeah, the couch. And I'm damned sorry about that, but I can't go back and redo it. But just because we…you know—" he gestured between the two of them with his hand "—doesn't guarantee we won't have a falling-out tomorrow. Or sooner. We're too volatile to add a personal relationship to the mix."

She was still back at the part about him redoing something. What would he have done differently? she wondered.

Don't go there, Jess.

"You have a point," she conceded. Her and Nick's battles had already caused strife—with her family, at least. Her parents had been wanting her to come to Dallas for a long time now, and she'd resisted, fought with them even.

Because of Nick.

He put his hands behind him on the dresser, leaned against the wood, let out a breath as though relieved that she understood.

"The truth is, you're important to me, Red. I think we could have a solid friendship, and I don't want to lose that possibility. Or put our folks and Coleman-Grayson's stockholders in a tight position if we screwed up."

Well. He could have used a better choice of words, but he made sense. It didn't alleviate the pang of rejection she felt—he'd satisfied his sexual curiosity and was now willing to move forward to the next item on the agenda.

Maybe that wasn't exactly fair or accurate, but the feeling stuck.

However, as a balm to the wound, he was offering her exactly what she'd wanted. To learn the absolute nitty-gritty about the business, those little details that weren't in a filing cabinet or spreadsheet somewhere. Details that were only inside his head, gleaned from experience.

Experience she didn't have as much of.

And she truly wanted to make a mark on the company, blaze a new trail. The idea percolating in the back of her mind, the research she'd been conducting for some time now, would benefit from more insider knowledge.

And that was the one thing she'd yet to accomplish since she'd come to Coleman-Grayson. Becoming an insider.

She took a breath, prayed she wasn't making a huge mistake, then stood and held out her hand.

"Deal. Twenty-four-seven. Where you go, I go—except to bed," she amended quickly. "Business only."

He took her hand, shook it, held it for a second longer than was necessary. For a minute, she thought he was going to debate the part about not going to bed.

Stunning her, scaring her, he raised her knuckles to his lips.

"Business only."

Chapter Nine

For the next two days, Jessica rode in to work with Nick. Since they'd more or less made a pact to tie themselves at the business hip, it seemed to make sense.

She'd had a bad patch going into his office that first morning after making love with him there, unable to look at the sofa without remembering, without desire tingling through her body. But she'd managed to bluff her way by feigning nonchalance.

There were definite drawbacks to spending this much time together, though.

The lack of privacy, for one. She had phone calls out on her project research and didn't particularly want to discuss them in front of Nick.

She wanted a better handle on the way he worked first. No sense missing something vital and having egg on her face with her first truly big presentation.

Nick held the door open for her as she preceded him into the air-conditioned lobby of a swanky uptown restaurant. They were having lunch with the president of

Amabella Cosmetics, then drinks later across town with executives of Damian Lease Management.

The hostess led them to a corner table where Amabella's young president was already seated, sipping on iced lemon water.

The woman stood. "Hey, handsome. Right on time as usual."

Nick grinned. "And you're early—as usual."

Jessica always had trouble getting used to Nick's easy smile. Around her, scowls were the norm. She forgot what the wattage of that smile did to his face. It gave *her* hot flashes.

"This is my associate, Jessica Coleman," Nick introduced, then held a chair out for her to sit. "Jess, this is Tina Lee. The brains behind Amabella Cosmetics."

"Nice to meet you, Jessica. Are you any relation to the Coleman part of Coleman-Grayson?"

"Yes. Randy Coleman's daughter...and major stockholder." She accepted Tina's handshake, then sat and placed the white linen napkin in her lap. Tina was a beautiful, petite woman full of energy and shrewd intelligence who laughed easily and projected a friendliness that put everyone at ease.

"Well, I'm honored," Tina said. "I get not one, but two of the top dogs today."

Jessica wasn't sure what her own role was here. Perhaps just to listen and learn? Did Nick expect her to offer opinions? Or simply absorb and familiarize herself with the various heads of the companies they invested in?

"I apologize that my associate couldn't make it today," Tina said. "There are always fires to put out, you know?"

"I hear you," Nick said. "Someone should invent a longer day."

"Heaven forbid!"

Jessica sat back and listened to the exchange, deciding in an instant that Tina Lee was someone who put her cards on the table. Jess was a pretty good judge of character, and she liked Tina instantly.

She had to admit that she was a bit surprised by the other woman's appearance. With a company named Amabella, she'd expected to meet a statuesque Frenchwoman. With her dark hair cut in a chic pageboy style and her distinctly Southern accent, it was quite obvious Tina was a Texas gal—or at least had been raised in the South.

She was also impressed with the way Nick responded to Tina. He gave her his full attention, didn't condescend or puff up his masculine feathers and try to act superior.

It made for an easy attitude around the lunch table.

Once they'd ordered and received their meals, Nick said, "Tell me more about the new campaign, Tina. How's it going?"

"Very well. We're so far under budget I keep thinking we've left something out."

"I doubt that."

Jessica silently seconded Nick's comment. It was

clear that this sharp businesswoman wouldn't miss anything vital.

"Do you have a sample of the colors you're offering?" Jessica asked. Nick had already briefed her on Amabella's latest product. A lip ink and gloss overlay that wouldn't rub or kiss off.

"Of course." Tina reached for her briefcase and passed Jessica a card with several rows of colors, beginning with white and ending with brown, and an impressive array of pinks and reds in between. "In fact, why don't you try the product before you finish eating? Nothing like a test run to sell you on an idea."

Jessica smiled. In this, she had the advantage over Nick. He probably wouldn't do an actual trial test himself, would have to take Tina at her word, as well as the scientific studies she had to back it up.

"This one's called Roux Shimmer. This color of red with a hint of coral will go fabulously with your features and bold hair."

Not giving a second thought to her primping at a business meeting, Jessica took out a mirror and tissue from her purse, removed what was left of her lipstick, then applied the liquid color to her lips.

"Careful," Tina cautioned. "You want to stay within the lines. Where you put it is where it stays."

"Not good for ladies with the shakes, huh?"

"Actually, we have a liner pen that'll outline and hide little mistakes."

Still, Jessica carefully followed the contours of her

lips. With her mouth open as though expecting a moist kiss, she expertly slashed beautiful color on her lips.

She noticed that Nick was watching. Spellbound.

Suddenly self-conscious, her hand trembled a bit.

Replacing the wand in the tube, she accepted the clear gloss Tina passed to her.

"This gives it shine and moisture," Tina explained.

"And it won't come off?"

"The gloss will need to be reapplied every so often, but the stain itself won't. Once you're done, you can eat and drink and make love or whatever you want and never have to give a thought to smears or pale lips."

Jessica gazed at Nick. He'd gone very quiet, wasn't eating his lemon chicken.

Instead, he was staring at her lips.

Oh, he had a very valid reason to do so, but it still made Jessica's heart beat faster. Was he thinking about making love? About *them* making love?

"Try it out," Tina offered enthusiastically. Unaware of the current zinging back and forth between Nick and Jessica, she added, "Perhaps Nick will be gallant and let you test it out on him."

Jessica raised a brow, nearly laughed at the struggle it took for him to keep his features schooled.

Poor guy. Trapped between two women sampling cosmetics.

He cleared his throat. "I'll just take your word for it."

Although he shifted an inch away from her, he still managed to look calm and cool. But Jessica could feel the vibration as he tapped his heel on the floor, betraying his nerves.

It was such a normal, human gesture, it actually surprised her.

Jessica raised the back of her hand to her lips and pressed, amazed that it came away clean, not an outline of a lip visible. ''Hey, this is great.''

Without conscious thought, she grabbed Nick's hand. ''Check it out.'' Puckering, she pressed her lips against the back of his hand.

Frown lines appeared on his forehead. He glanced quickly at Tina as though checking to see if she'd heard the crack of electricity that had arced at the touch of lips against hand.

Jessica tried to act as though they were merely business associates, as though her lips hadn't sipped at more intimate parts of his body less than two days ago. She hoped to heaven her eyes didn't betray her.

She took a breath, handed the samples back to Tina and reined her mind back where it belonged. ''You've got a winner here. Did you say you're under budget?''

''Tremendously.''

''Mind if I make a couple of suggestions for you to kick around?''

''Shoot.''

''Offer a blue and green shade, as well.''

''Blue and green?'' Nick asked incredulously.

''Yes.'' She dismissed his skepticism, keeping her gaze on Tina, who she could see was quite interested.

"Several shades, in fact. And glitter. Especially in the silver, gold and blue shades."

"From a man's point of view—"

"I love it!" Tina said, both of them ignoring Nick's attempted input.

Nick took a sip of water. The idea had been to show Jessica what went on at luncheon business meetings, but somehow he'd lost control of the floor. It was a gender thing, he decided, due to the particular subject matter.

Still, glitter? Blue and green glitter? On lips?

Jessica's favorite word, criminy, flashed through his mind.

"It's all the rage at clubs, Nick," Jessica said, absently patting his thigh, nearly sending him straight up out of his chair.

Hell on fire, he never knew what to expect when he got together with Jessica Coleman. And what kind of clubs did she go to, anyway?

"I can tell you right now it's not going to go over big with the men. Who wants to kiss blue or green glittery lips?"

"Who cares if it goes over with the men? Women buy these cosmetics for themselves—not to impress guys."

"Then why do the advertisers focus on sex and innuendo?" he countered.

"Because women want to feel sexy," Tina said. "For themselves, like Jessica said."

"Trust me, Nick. Tina and I know what we're talking about here.'' She took a bite of her veal picatta, slowly, erotically dragging her full lips over the tines of the fork.

Nick swallowed the groan that clawed at his throat, twisted in his belly.

''Look. Not even a trace came off. I need some of this stuff.''

The open awe on her face enchanted him.

Tina handed over two tubes, a color and a gloss. ''With those fabulous lips, we ought to put you in the advertisement.''

Jess laughed. ''No thanks. I'd just as soon stay behind the scenes. Besides, with a name like Amabella, you need a gorgeous French model. How'd you settle on the name, anyway? I mean, you're obviously not...'' Her words trailed off as though she realized whatever she'd been about to say might sound insulting.

''French?'' Tina guessed with a quiet laugh. ''No, born and raised in Lubbock, Texas, actually. But my great-great-grandmother married a Frenchman and named my great-grandmother Amabella. I thought it was so classy and perfect for a cosmetic line.''

''It means lovable,'' Jessica commented absently, then glanced at Nick. ''I looked it up.'' She turned back to Tina. ''You know, you could do something with that.''

Nick could practically see the wheels of her mind begin to turn faster and faster. It fascinated him, and he laid aside his fork to see where she'd go with the conversation.

"A gimmick," she said, punctuating the word with her fork. "Shift your focus, perhaps. Come up with a signature line of perfume. I could put you in touch with a friend of mine in France. He's a genius at personalizing fragrance."

"You've been to France?" Nick asked. And who was this Frenchman?

She glanced at him, gave a saucy smile. "Yes. Missed that detail about me, hmm?"

Yes, he had. He imagined there was a world of details he'd missed about Jessica Coleman.

"I've been admiring your scent," Tina said. "Did your friend do it for you?"

"Mmm. Isn't it great? It's called JRC—stands for Jessica Rose Coleman. No one else has it. I wanted something flirty, but light, like walking barefoot through flowers in a spring meadow."

He was pretty sure she had her shoes on, but he still had an urge to look beneath the table to see if she'd kicked them off.

"Back to the gimmick, though," she continued. "Package the lipstick along with the perfume. You say your cost ratio on the lip ink is practically nothing. You can afford to do a free-gift sort of thing, absorb it in the price of the perfume. Then when both products take off, you'll still have stayed within the budget for your initial capital outlay, but you stand to make double the profit or more."

She wrote a name on the back of her business card and passed it to Tina. "Here's my friend's name and number. Give him a call. Paint a picture for him, and you'll be amazed at what he'll come up with. Maybe play on the meaning of the name—lovable. Playful. Sexy."

"From young girls to grandmothers," Nick mused, caught up in the animation of her words and gestures, able to see the direction she was going.

"Exactly. The glitter and wild colors for the lips will draw in the younger set. The ease, staying power and good old standby shades will appeal to older generations. And the perfume, something light and fresh can work for a wide range of ages. Innocence through experience."

Innocence through experience. Suddenly Nick pictured an image of Jessica and him. Innocence, experience, lovable, playful, sexy...

Man alive, he had to keep his mind on business and off pleasures—pleasures he couldn't allow himself to have.

Tina was writing notes as fast as she could, her sun-dried-tomato-and-artichoke salad forgotten.

Nick, too, had forgotten to eat. Jessica was the only one making a dent in her meal.

Ideas just seemed to pour out of her, suggestions that were innovative and made good business sense. She didn't advocate spending huge amounts of money. Just restructuring and using available resources to go a step farther—a step better.

She amazed him. She had a head for business, a knack that few possessed. It came so easily to her, too.

Usually in meetings like this, ideas were thrown on the table, discussed and only a fraction of them deemed viable.

Jessica hadn't missed the mark yet.

He was proud.

And he was also just the slightest bit threatened.

Oddly enough, at that moment, he felt obsolete, and it wasn't a position he liked being in; it wasn't a feeling he liked having.

It shamed him, in fact. She'd just proposed an idea that would amount to millions, benefit all of them.

So why did it seem as though he was about to lose all control—both personally and business-wise?

THE DAY HAD BEEN productive, and Jessica was riding high on adrenaline.

She hadn't meant to take over the meeting at lunch, but the subject matter had been right up her alley. More so than Nick's, although he'd contributed plenty of intelligent input. It was his sharp mind, his easy way with people that impressed her so, made her want to emulate him, learn from him.

She tended to go on emotions, and he looked at the logic of a matter.

Both were different ways of operating, and both had merit, but Nick's way was definitely safer. She realized that impulsiveness had to be tempered in business.

Especially when millions of dollars were at stake.

The afternoon meeting with the leasing company had been an eye-opener, as well. In that session, Nick had been in his element.

And she'd been content to sit back and listen, watch him in action, admire the drive and determination that had gotten him to where he was today.

She'd also realized that was what had been missing for her at Coleman-Grayson.

Being in the inner loop.

Business lunches and meeting with clients and associates was how most deals got closed, how most deals were found out about in the first place.

He was as good as his promise, easing her into that inner loop, where a word here or there could start and close a deal within weeks—months before the general public or smaller investor even knew something was in the wind.

One thing was for sure, Jessica thought. All this eating and socializing would take a toll on the fit of her clothes if she wasn't careful. She'd have to increase her swimming laps.

She knew how Nick stayed in such fabulous shape—by going to a gym three times a week before work. Jessica, since she'd been hitching a ride with him, had tagged along.

And drooled a bit, she had to admit.

Although he'd offered to sign her up with a membership through the company, she'd declined. Going to the gym was too disciplined for her personality. She needed more freedom, more spontaneity. That was why water appealed to her—the freedom it afforded her.

Back at Nick's house that evening, debating whether to choose the lake or the swimming pool, she looked up as Nick came down the stairs.

He was dressed in glove-soft jeans that were conditioned to the contours of his body, and a black T-shirt that hugged his strong torso.

Casual. She didn't often see him that way.

"You on your way out?" she asked.

"Yeah."

If he had a date, she was going to feel really stupid. Still, she didn't like the idea that he might be ducking her.

The man was a workaholic. She wouldn't be surprised if he planned to conduct business—just in a more relaxed setting than she'd seen him in so far.

"So, where are we going?"

"We?"

"Twenty-four-seven, remember? Unless, of course, this might end up in the threesome classification. I know that's just about every man's fantasy, but you'd have to count me out."

He reached for the doorknob of the coat closet and missed. Glancing at her sharply, he shook his head.

"I prefer one woman at a time."

"That's a relief. So what about our twenty-four-seven pact?"

He sighed, the sound holding more than a little edge.

"Look, if you want to come with me, just say so and get in the car."

"Why, I'd love to. Thank you so much for asking." She gave him a cheeky smile, snagged her purse off the hall table and followed him outside, slipping into the black Mercedes before he had a chance to change his mind.

She wondered if he noticed how nicely she'd done that—gotten into the car without arguing about who would drive.

"You never said where we're going."

"Just sit there and you'll find out."

Jessica loved adventure, so it didn't bother her to sit back and let him lead the way—or steer them, as it were.

Since he wore jeans, she was fairly confident that her denim skirt, capped-sleeve top and sandals were appropriate. Even if they weren't, Jessica had enough confidence not to worry about her clothes. The only time she got a little testy, or slightly self-conscious, was when people blatantly stared at her generously endowed chest and disregarded the rest of her.

They drove through the countryside, then into the outskirts of Dallas. Storm clouds that had been gathering strength all day brewed overhead, obliterating the stars.

She noticed that Nick was nervous and unusually quiet. Oh, she was used to his bouts of surliness, but this was different. She had an idea if she asked him about it, he'd take her head off, so she simply sat quietly and absorbed the ambiance of the night and the cool interior of the car.

When he pulled into the parking lot of a small nightclub, Jessica leaned forward to read the sign above the door, which was lit with miniature white lights.

"We're going honky-tonking? My, my, you *are* a surprise."

He parked around back, then climbed out of the car and grabbed a guitar case from the trunk.

Jessica frowned. "What in the world is that?"

"What does it look like?" For once, Nick didn't appear so confident.

He seemed...embarrassed? Unsure?

"Is that yours or are you dropping it off for someone?"

"It's mine."

"Are you part of the entertainment?"

"Yes." He snapped the word as though waiting for her to make an issue of it.

She held up her hands. "Well, aren't you just full of surprises." She hooked her arm through his and tugged him toward the door. "I'm looking forward to this."

Chapter Ten

It took a while for Nick to relax, but the music and familiar vibration of the guitar strings beneath his fingertips worked their magic.

All the while he played, Nick was excruciatingly aware of Jessica. She was far from a wallflower, didn't appear as though she'd ever met a stranger. She walked into a room and lit it up with her presence.

Women looked at her with envy and men's gazes followed her with yearning. She didn't even seem to be aware of it. She didn't flaunt or act coy or unapproachable. She laughed and eased right into the flow of the crowd, gathering admirers in her wake.

Sitting on a stool on the stage, he played the notes of the country-and-western ballad by rote, feeling the rhythm as though it was second nature. In a way it was. He'd been drawn to music ever since he was a boy.

He didn't deliberately hide this part of his life; he just didn't advertise it. It was a relief after the long hours of cutthroat business, a place to simply not think, to let the frivolous side of him emerge.

He'd been responsible for so long, since he was a kid. If he'd told his family he wanted to be a performer in a band, they'd probably have suggested he see a doctor, suspected aliens had invaded his body and replaced the man they knew as their son.

The singer got the crowd going when Nick nodded and led the group into a fast rendition of the Charlie Daniels Band hit, "The Devil Went Down to Georgia." It was the kind of music that made people want to dance or ride a mechanical bull. Sonny, the fiddle player, skipped his bow over the strings in an impressive, lightning-fast show. Nick picked up the pace on his acoustical guitar, adjusting the microphone to better project the tones.

He saw Jessica whirl around in delight and salute him with her beer bottle. He grinned. This was why he did this—for the thrill, the adrenaline rush, the entertainment.

And probably for his ego, too.

Without waiting for a partner, she headed for the dance floor and joined a group of women already doing a complicated line dance.

The movements of her body made him sweat, but Nick needed to concentrate on the chords of the fast-paced tune.

He did wonder, though, if their positions had been reversed and he'd been the one left to mill about alone, if he'd have joined in as easily as Jessica did.

He doubted it. That was another of the differences

between them. He thought about things first. Jessica acted on impulse and emotion.

JESSICA WAS HAVING the time of her life. She absolutely loved the energy in places like this. And she was seeing a whole new side to Nick.

My gosh, he was so handsome it gave her a fluttery feeling just to look at him. Watching him perform with the stage lights gleaming off his dark hair gave her a sense of pride, of…importance. Because she'd come with him.

And she'd be going home with him.

Criminy, she was starting to think like a groupie.

It was a blast.

Distracted, she kicked, instead of scuffed, and ended up out of step and nearly caused a pile-up on the dance floor. Laughing, she got back in the rhythm, then gave up when the tune got so fast it made her dizzy.

She saw one of the women who'd lived at her old apartment building and went over to her table. It had only been a week since the fire, but it seemed like a lifetime. So much had happened.

For one, she'd found out what it felt like to truly become a woman. To experience an intimacy she'd only imagined.

"Hey, y'all."

"Jessica!" Myrna said. "It's great to see you."

"Did you find a place to stay?"

"Yes, Debra and I rented a small house in town." Myrna motioned to the woman sitting next to her.

"Buildings with more than one floor make us a little shaky, if you know what I mean. How about you? Where are you living now?"

"With him." Jessica nodded toward the stage without looking. The music had stopped now, and she assumed they were deciding what to play next. "The serious-looking guitar player."

"Get out."

"Scout's honor."

"My gosh, he's a dream."

She grinned. "Actually, we're just friends. Business associates."

"Yeah, right."

"Really," Jessica said.

"Then introduce me, because he's coming our way. And if you're stupid enough to pass up a hunk like that, I'll surely step up to the plate."

Jessica felt a surge of jealousy, and it annoyed her. She didn't have any claims on Nick Grayson—even though he'd been her first lover.

He'd made it clear that a relationship between them was too risky. And as much as that bothered her, she realized he had a valid point.

He stopped next to her. "Nick, this is Myrna Finch and her friend Debra."

Myrna got up and moved right in next to Nick, letting him know she was interested and available. Jessica wondered why she'd ever liked the woman in the first place. Myrna had tiny little hips and perfectly round, perky breasts the size of small grapefruits. It was clear she wasn't wearing a bra.

In contrast, Jessica's hips filled out her denim skirt—very nicely, she had to admit—but her melon-size breasts prevented her from being described as slim. And they definitely wouldn't stand at attention without the aid of a good underwire bra.

"Nice to meet you," Nick said politely. Jessica backed up to give him room, but he moved with her.

"Surely you're not done for the night," Myrna cooed, glancing at the guitar case he held in his hand.

"Actually, I am. This is my hobby. My real job requires I get my beauty sleep."

He was so smooth, disengaging himself from Myrna's clutches without insulting her. Jessica was impressed.

"Ready?" he asked, looking at her.

"Whenever you are. You're driving."

He put a hand under her elbow and guided her toward the door. "And a good thing, too. You nearly caused a wreck out on the dance floor."

She giggled. "It's funny how one person teaches a line dance one way, and you go to another place and they do it totally differently."

"Yeah, they have a gal who comes in on Tuesdays and gives free lessons."

"Guess she's not the same one who gave lessons at the club in Austin where I learned."

"Guess not."

The air smelled of rain. The temperature had cooled

a bit, but humidity still hung heavy in the air and the pavement was practically steaming. Still it was a relief from the smoky interior of the bar.

She got in the car. "So how long have you been doing this gig?"

"A couple of years. I used to come in to hear Sonny play his fiddle. The guy smokes on that instrument."

She noticed the excitement in his voice when he talked about music and his friends. He was like that about business, as well. Had she totally misjudged him? Did she look so hard for the bad that she completely missed the clues of all the good?

Nick Grayson was much deeper than she'd thought. He wasn't stuffy. He'd proved that tonight. He was exciting.

And not interested, she reminded herself.

"Do your folks ever come listen to you play?"

"I've never invited them, no."

"Do they even know?"

He shrugged and turned on the windshield wipers when the first drops of rain started. Thunder rolled in the distance and lightning flashed. "Maybe Chase has told them. They've never mentioned it."

"Doesn't that bother you?"

"Why would it? If I wanted them in the audience, I'd invite them. Frankly, Jess, I need a part of my life that's separate from the business, from my family. I give everything I am to Coleman-Grayson. Sometimes I just need something for me."

Dear God, he was human, after all. When had she

started viewing him as some sort of robot? A tin man who doesn't feel? He was like everyone else in the world.

Jessica hated it when she misjudged people. She hated it when she judged in the first place. It wasn't fair.

But with Nick, how could she have helped it? The friction between them, the friction that had been there for years, had shaped her opinions.

They'd probably shaped his opinions of her, too.

The windshield wipers were slashing in earnest at the downpour now. Nick pulled the Mercedes into the six-car garage and shut the automatic door behind them.

Since they'd always parked outside before, she hadn't had occasion to see this part of his house. Sure enough, he had plenty of cars. Aside from the Mercedes, he owned a convertible Corvette, a Suburban and a mean-looking Harley-Davidson.

"Well, heck, Nick," she said as they got out of the car, "if I'd known you had that Harley, I'd have taken you up on the offer you made for the use of transportation, rather than leasing the Tahoe."

"Oh, no. I offered a car. Not the bike."

"I always knew you were sexist," she teased.

He grinned. "If you play your cards right, I might take you for a ride sometime."

The unintended sexual innuendo hit them both at the same time. She looked at him. He looked at her.

Jessica had trouble drawing a breath or walking straight. "Business only," she reminded him.

"Yeah." There was a world of disappointment in that single word. Jessica felt it, too.

They continued on into the kitchen. Through the window, illuminated by the yard lighting, she could see rain pouring into the swimming pool, the waterfall rushing even swifter. The normally placid lake rippled in the summer storm as the powerboat still moored at the dock bobbed.

"Do you have a cover for the boat?"

He swore. "I forgot about that."

"Yikes, a guy who forgets about a toy? My my, you *have* been working too hard. Although, I've got to say, tonight was very inspiring. Who knew you had it in you?"

"How long is it going to take for this to get around the office?"

She shrugged. "As long as it takes for you to tell folks, I guess. Come on, let's go cover that boat." If he wanted a piece of his life just for himself, she wasn't going to take that from him.

"You don't have to help. It's pouring out there."

"Duh. I'm already wet and there's nothing I love better than a warm rain."

"Sticky, you mean," he said, and held the back door open for her. "The mosquitoes will carry you off."

"Not me. They're not attracted to my skin."

"No brains," he muttered.

"What was that?" She'd heard him, all right, but wondered if he'd repeat it.

"I said go rains."

She punched him on the shoulder. "Thanks, anyway."

"You're welcome."

Squealing as the rain plastered her hair to her head, she took off running, kicking her sandals off on the back patio, feeling the wet slick grass and mud ooze between her toes and splash on her ankles.

Nick caught up with her, but waited until he was on the dock to peel off his boots.

"Where's the cover?"

"Right over there."

"Oh. The boathouse. I was picturing a canvas cover."

Thunder boomed. Nick glanced up at the sky. "Come on. Let's move."

He vaulted into the boat and started up the powerful engine as Jessica untied the ropes and jumped in behind him. "There's a flashlight under the seat," he called.

She lifted the leather seat and retrieved it. "This isn't a flashlight. It's a beacon!" The million-candle-power spotlight lit up the dock and surrounding water.

She shone the beam about and laughed with unrestrained joy.

"You're a lunatic," he said with a grin. "Doesn't that lightning scare you?"

"Hey, if our butts get fried, it'll be your fault for leaving your toys out."

"I told you to stay in the house."

"I promise not to sue if I get zapped on your property."

He gunned the engine of the boat, nearly knocking her over. She saw a smirk on his face.

"I'm in a hurry."

"Yeah, well, watch where you're going. You're liable to wreck us right into the side of the boathouse. Cut a little more to the left."

"I could drive this boat blindfolded."

"Tough guy." Using the flashlight, she watched the front of the boat as he eased it into the shelter. Rain beat on the tin roof, coming down harder now. Another clap of thunder rattled the shedlike structure.

The boathouse was about the size of a two-car garage, with a wooden U-shaped platform that seemed to have been built to the specifications of this particular boat.

Fishing tackle hung on the walls, as well as life vests and skiing equipment. The smell of gasoline and oil mingled with the fresh smell of rain.

Jessica hopped onto the platform and hooked a rope to the cleats, securing the front of the boat, then went to the back to do the same.

"You make a pretty good first mate," Nick said.

She was sure he'd meant it as a compliment on her boating skills, but for some reason, the words *first mate* translated to *wife* in her mind.

Criminy, Jessica. Have you lost your ever-lovin' mind?

"No need to tie us off tight, though. There's a hydraulic lift beneath the boat."

"Well, aren't you special." She loosened the ropes and pushed wet hair out of her face.

He shut off the engine and climbed out over the bow. Going to a switch on the wall, he pushed a lever that produced a whining sound. In a few seconds, the boat started rising out of the water.

"Wait," Jessica said, holding up a hand. She leaned down and checked the underside of the boat. "Take it down a notch. You're not on straight."

He lowered the boat and she shoved it over to align it with the steel guides. "Okay, now go up again."

The mechanism whined and the boat was slowly lifted out of the water.

"Perfect," he said.

As she straightened, the powerful flashlight beam landed on Nick.

Yes, she thought. Perfect.

All he wore was a pair of jeans with a belt. He'd taken off his shoes and socks on the dock, and evidently when she wasn't looking, he'd removed his black T-shirt.

Tremors skittered through her body. Lightning flashed and she could have sworn the hair on her arms stood up. The electrical pull between them was hard to deny.

My gosh, she didn't think she'd ever seen a more handsome man in her entire life. And she'd grown up with three men who'd been *very* lucky in the gene department.

Clearing her throat, she angled the light away from him. One good thing—she'd probably half blinded him, so he wouldn't know she'd been almost panting.

"The storm's getting closer," she said inanely.

"Sounds like it."

"How crazy would it be to make a mad dash for the house?"

He picked up his discarded shirt and wiped his chest, started walking toward her on the wooden boards. "Pretty crazy."

"Well." She turned, folded her arms across her chest, then switched off the light she still held in her hands. Lightning streaked across the sky, illuminating the lake and the interior of the shed. "I suppose we could get comfy in the boat if we had to."

"We could." He came up beside her, reached into a cabinet over her head and got down a towel, which he handed to her. "Or we could just sit here and watch the show. It's moving pretty fast. I imagine it'll be over soon."

She wrapped the towel around her shoulders. "I imagine."

Nick dropped a towel to the damp boards and wiped up the puddles left by their bare feet. "Want me to lower the boat?"

"No. The floor's fine." She made sure she stayed several feet back from the open doors, but positioned herself so she could still see the glorious show of nature.

It took a minute to figure out how to get comfortable wearing a snug denim skirt. She hiked it up enough to sit, but to retain a modicum of modesty, she had to lean sideways, propped on one arm.

Nick reached for another towel, dropped it in her lap. "No sense cutting off your circulation."

"Thanks." She crossed her legs and used the towel as a blanket over her lap. Nick lowered himself next to her, one knee cocked, the other lying straight, nearly touching her thigh.

Shirtless and shoeless, he gave her goose bumps.

"So tell me about this Frenchman," he said casually.

She smiled. "I spent a summer in France. I met him when I did one of those tours in Grasse at the perfume factory. He was very…charming."

"Were you in love with him?"

She was a little surprised he'd asked that question. He knew she'd been a virgin up until a few nights ago. "No. We were just pals."

"Have you ever been in love?"

Jessica went very still. The words *Yes, practically all my life—with you* echoed in her mind. "No. How about you?"

"No."

This was the oddest conversation. "I spoiled you for other women when I was thirteen." She elbowed him lightly in the ribs. "Admit it."

"Must have."

She doubted it. But teasing him seemed to be the only smart way to curb the seriousness.

"Can I ask you a personal question?" He didn't look at her, kept staring out at the night.

So much for keeping things light. "Seems you've been doing nothing *but* asking personal questions. What else do you want to know?"

"Why me? You waited twenty-five years to give yourself to a man. What tipped the scales the other night?"

She took a breath. "It wasn't planned. I hadn't deliberately waited for you in particular. Emotions just seemed to overrule good sense."

"That's just it. Haven't you ever been in a situation like that before? Where emotions overruled?"

"I guess not." Obviously. "What do you want me to say, Nick? I know where we stand. I know how you feel. Heck, I half agree with you about personal stuff mucking up business relationships. It's risky. But we're both adults. I'm not looking for, nor have I asked you for a committed relationship, so there's no cause for concern on my part. If you're feeling guilty, that is."

"I *am* feeling guilty."

Her fists tightened around the towel in her lap. "If we weren't in the middle of a lightning storm, I'd knock you into the water for that."

"For what?"

"Assuming responsibility for my feelings. I'm a big girl, Nick. I don't blame you or hold you responsible.

It takes two to tango, as they say. And I, for one, immensely enjoyed myself on that couch.''

There. She'd rendered him speechless. She hadn't realized she was going to say that, was glad that the lack of light in the boathouse hid the blush she could feel staining her skin.

He shifted toward her, tipped her chin up with a single finger. The tension in the humid air was thick enough to slice with a wet noodle.

His palm slid up the side of her face, his fingers sifted through her hair. And all the while, he simply stared at her, held her with the intensity of his gaze.

Jessica didn't know what to do. Didn't know how to react. Was he going to disregard all his reservations and pick up where they'd left off?

Was she going to let him?

She let out the breath she'd been holding, turned her head, breaking the spell. The thunder was moving off into the distance now, the lightning still streaking, but miles away.

She stood and went to the edge of the open boathouse doors, gazed up at the stormy sky. Clouds still brewed, but the threat wasn't anywhere nearly as bad as the threat in the dark boathouse.

''Do we need to check on the horses before we go in?''

''No,'' he said from right behind her. ''Russ will have taken care of them.

She nodded. She'd been at Nick's house for a week now, and she hadn't yet made it out to the barn to meet the man who lived in an apartment over the tack room and took care of the horses and stable. She hadn't ridden a horse or gone out for a boat ride as she'd wanted to, either.

Moving the powerboat a few yards didn't count as a ride.

"Well, then, I guess we should get out of here before we get in trouble."

"Yeah. You're probably right."

Interesting that neither one of them put any enthusiasm into their words.

Chapter Eleven

On Friday afternoon, Jessica took off early to meet with the insurance people about the destroyed apartment building—both as a representative of Coleman-Grayson and as a former tenant. Most owners didn't carry insurance that covered their tenants' contents, usually leaving it up to each individual to obtain coverage on his or her own. But Coleman-Grayson supplied it as a perk.

Jessica was happy that her neighbors would be reimbursed for their losses. Not everyone was in as fortunate a position as her, having a cushion of funds, as well as family and company backing.

Rather than returning to work so late in the day, she drove to Nick's house and was contemplating taking a swim when she saw his car pull into the driveway.

He came in the front door and set his briefcase on the hall table.

"You're home early," she said. "Checking up on me for playing hooky?"

He shook his head. "How'd it go with the insurance people?"

"We're all covered. I signed the forms and the company's contacting the rest of the tenants."

"Good." He shifted from foot to foot, a nervousness she wasn't used to seeing.

"Did you need something?" she asked. Well, that was a loaded question.

"Yeah. I've got this banquet to attend. Do you want to go with me?"

"When?"

"Tonight."

Her jaw dropped. What a guy.

"Nice of you to give a person advance warning." She appreciated him keeping up his end of the twenty-four-seven pact, but there were certain things a girl didn't want to be spontaneous about—usually things that involved deciding what to wear.

Before he could take back the invitation, she said, "Of course I'd be happy to go. I don't have anything to wear to a banquet, though, so exactly how much time do I have to shop?"

"You haven't been upstairs yet?"

"No. I just got home a few minutes ago. Why?"

He shoved his hands in his pockets. "I got you something you might like."

He could have knocked her over with a hummingbird feather. Surprise raised her voice an octave. "You bought me a present?"

"Yeah. It was a weak moment."

She laughed, delighted. She'd probably hate it, or not be able to get it zipped.

Most guys didn't have a clue how to shop for a woman. But the gesture touched her.

Impulsively she went up on tiptoe and kissed him on the cheek. "Thank you in advance."

His eyes widened, but she went upstairs before he had a chance to react, before they could get caught up in a tide of emotions they both knew better than to dip a toe in.

The box sat in the middle of the satin bedspread on her bed in the guest room. She recognized the name of the store.

How had he gotten it in here without her seeing it? And when? Then she remembered that she'd taken her own car to the office this morning, had actually gloated because she'd been ready to leave before him.

Pulling off her shoes, she walked barefoot over the plush ivory carpet, slowly removed the gold ribbon and lifted the lid of the box. Her fingers trembled for no good reason.

Inside was the red dress she'd tried on that first day at the mall—the one that had cost the earth.

Omigosh. He'd bought it for her.

Out of habit, she checked the tag. It was her size. She knew it would fit. And so had he. He'd already seen her in it.

This was the first time in her life a man had bought her clothing. She was touched and strangely excited.

She lifted the dress and draped it over the bedspread.

This particular article of clothing screamed sex. And that was a road they both should know better than to travel.

Still, she went into the bathroom and soaked in a soothingly scented bath, carefully shaved her legs, then dried off and creamed her skin. Her signature JRC scent filled the bathroom and flowed out to the bedroom when she opened the door.

It struck her that this was just like getting ready for a date.

But it wasn't a date.

Even though he'd bought her a dress, she was only…only what?

His date.

Oh, stop it.

LUCKILY SHE HAD silver shoes and a matching handbag to go with the dress—she'd bought both on her shoe-shopping spree at the mall.

Fastening a delicate diamond pendant around her neck, she picked up her handbag and made her way toward the stars.

The nerves fluttering in her stomach were new and out of character. *It's no big deal,* she told herself. *Just walk down the darn stairs.*

She was halfway down when she spotted him. He wore a black suit and white shirt. He looked absolutely wonderful. She wanted just to take a moment and stare at him, but at that instant, he turned.

And went utterly still.

Hands in his pants pockets, he watched her descend the remaining stairs, his gaze like a caress.

Jessica reached up to fuss with her hair, then dropped her hand when she remembered it wasn't flowing over her shoulders as usual. She'd piled it on her head, a few long strands left strategically loose.

Some might call it a messy look. Jessica preferred to think of it as sexy.

And evidently so did Nick. He looked...stunned.

She had an urge to tug at the bodice of the dress, see if the delicate spaghetti straps would adjust a bit higher. She was modestly covered. Still, with her measurements, that didn't mean a whole lot.

"You took my breath away when I saw you in that dress at the store," he said, his voice raspy. "I don't think I can find the words for what I'm feeling right now."

Her heart jumped. She saw the genuine appreciation in his chocolate-brown eyes. She felt like Cinderella—except her prince had come to pick her up for the ball.

She cleared her throat and gave a curtsy, then casually walked past him into the foyer.

She wasn't going to buy into the fairy tale.

"Thank you. For the dress and the compliment. You're looking pretty sharp yourself."

His lips twitched. "Tough girl."

Darn his hide for seeing through her. "That's me." She reached for the front door, needing to get out into the fresh air before she changed her mind and decided to seduce him, instead.

He put his hand over hers on the doorknob and she literally jumped.

"Allow me."

There was something different about him tonight. A certain banked seductiveness. Nothing overt that she could put her finger on. It was an aura, a feeling that teased her nerve endings, made her tremble.

He touched her elbow to steady her as they went down the front steps, then held the car door open for her.

Getting the full gentlemanly treatment like this was throwing her off balance.

What happened to his admonitions about not mixing business with pleasure? The look in his eyes definitely telegraphed pleasure—or the promise of it.

She took a breath, ordered herself to be calm, remember who they were, why she was going with him in the first place. She was staying at his house. It would have been rude of him not to invite her.

Not to mention going back on his word.

"I assume your invitation said you could bring a guest, didn't it?" She needed to know if her presence would be considered proper etiquette or party crashing.

"Yes. Especially since I'm the guest of honor."

"Excuse me?"

"I'm involved with Big Brothers of America. They're presenting me with an award."

For a minute she simply gaped at him. "I've got to say, you surprise the heck out of me at every turn. You play in a honky-tonk band and volunteer in the community. And here I thought you were all work and no play."

"Why, Jess, have you been trying to pigeonhole me?"

"Yes. And I've a feeling I've done you a grave disservice."

He shrugged. "It's no big deal, really. I've been a volunteer for the Big Brothers of America program for about five years now. They're honoring a project I started to keep delinquent kids off the streets and drugs, to teach them a skill."

"What project is that?"

"Boys Town Bakery."

"You're kidding! You own that?"

"I funded it, yes."

"Why a bakery?"

"Because most street-tough kids think baking's a female thing. When they get in there and learn that some of the most famous chefs in the world are men and the kind of honest living they make at it, they change their minds. And baking is art, creation. A guy can decorate a cake and exercise his creativity, rather than marking up walls with graffiti."

"Do you help out teaching them to bake? Provide recipes?" She couldn't picture it.

"No. I delegate that. But I've baked a few cakes right alongside the boys. I'm an ace with a tube of icing and decorating tip."

"Amazing." That was the only word she could think of.

They pulled up to the front entrance of an elegant hotel. The valet rushed to open her door and offered a hand to assist her out of the car. In seconds Nick was beside her, offering his arm.

The Cinderella image popped into her mind again. Slipping her arm through his, she breathed deeply and said, "Well, here we go."

"Red?"

"Yes?"

"If I forget to tell you later, you were the most beautiful woman in the room."

His brown eyes shone with sincerity and appreciation, leaving little doubt that he did indeed believe she was beautiful.

Jessica wasn't normally a woman who needed her ego stroked, but his words touched her in a way she couldn't quite explain.

"Thank you."

FOR THE NEXT several hours, Jessica tried not to let her surprise show. She watched Nick, so smooth and suave. Every other woman in the room, young and old, watched him, too. He was a man who inspired fantasies, no matter what a woman's age.

After a buffet and brief presentation, Nick took the microphone and gave a short speech about the pleasure he derived from giving back to the community.

Jessica thought about the company slogan on the office wall—People who invest in people and the community—and about how he'd taken on two companies for the sake of friendships.

He was a man who didn't hesitate to help. The reaction of people in this room tonight proved it.

She'd always viewed him as a no-nonsense, high-powered businessman who expected everyone to live up to his standards. She hadn't considered how much he gave of himself.

Even to her. Oh, it was a fairly recent change of direction, but nevertheless, he was doing her a favor, helping her learn the ropes at Coleman-Grayson.

A company he'd been practically running single-handedly. Did he view it as training his competition? She didn't like to think of them as competitors.

He stepped down off the stage amid thunderous applause and stopped to shake hands with a group of men. The sight of him, so tall and strong and self-assured, so incredibly handsome in his perfectly tailored black suit, sent butterflies winging in her stomach. Butterflies she recognized as desire.

But what if by some horrible chance, things did end up going sour between them? Embarking on this career was the most important thing she'd ever done in her life. She loved the work, had so many ideas and plans for the future.

Her life was only beginning.

What would happen if she was forced to choose?

If *he* was forced to choose?

The fact that her family owned fifty-one percent of

the voting stock could easily become a nasty issue between them if a disagreement arose.

She put the thought out of her mind when the musicians struck up a slow tune.

Nick excused himself from the group of men he'd been talking with and came toward her. He stopped in front of her and held out his hand. "May I have this dance?"

"Absolutely." Propelled by riotous emotions, she went into his arms as though she belonged there. At that moment she couldn't even begin to imagine a rift between them.

She was simply borrowing trouble. *He* was borrowing trouble.

Now how did she go about convincing him of that?

And guarding her heart at the same time?

His thighs brushed against hers, and her stockings whispered against the material of his pants. Her hand felt small in his. He smelled delicious.

"You smell great," he said.

She chuckled. "I was just thinking the same thing about you."

"You like my soap?"

"Mmm-hmm." She imagined it was more than soap, but she couldn't place the scent. It was uniquely Nick.

"Your Frenchman did a good job matching your fragrance to you." His words were murmured against her temple, his warm breath stirring the tendrils of hair that hung loose around her face from her updo.

"Should we take off our shoes? Pretend we're walking through wildflowers?'' That was the description that had been the basis for the formula.

''I think we can use our imaginations. Might raise eyebrows if we start disrobing.''

''Kicking off shoes is hardly disrobing.''

Although that was how it had all started in his office last week. She'd taken off her shoes. Had some wine. Then they'd both been naked. Well, nearly naked. She hadn't ever really discarded her skirt.

''Maybe we better play it safe,'' he said.

''Do you care so much what others think of you?''

He gazed down at her. The next thing she knew she was standing on her own on the dance floor and he was leaning down to slip off his shoes.

She sputtered out a giggle. ''Nick!''

He grinned up at her, then eased her silver slides off her feet. She gripped his shoulders so she wouldn't fall. The whole crazy display took only seconds. But in those seconds, people watched and smiled.

And Jessica nearly melted into a puddle—right here in front of the Big Brothers of America crowd.

He tossed their shoes to the edge of the dance floor, then, in his sock feet, stood before her and opened his arms, inviting her to finish the dance. ''How's this?''

''You're crazy.''

''At least that's better than being stuffy.''

Her hand eased around his neck, toyed with his collar and the fine hair that brushed it. ''I should have never said that about you. Especially before checking my facts. I'm sorry.''

"Jessica Coleman's apologizing?" His voice rang with false astonishment.

She grinned and tweaked his hair. "I've been known to do it a time or two."

He tightened his arm around her waist and twirled her into a series of turns. Her feet whispered against the marble floor. If it wasn't for his secure hold on her, she might have slipped.

"Have you ever danced without your shoes in public?" she asked.

"Never. Think we'll start a trend?"

"I believe the trend's already acceptable. I rarely go to a wedding or social where at least some of the women don't take off their shoes."

"If you all wouldn't buy them two sizes too small, that wouldn't be a problem."

"Who buys shoes two sizes too small?"

"I thought that was a female thing. Wanting smaller feet."

"Well, I can't speak for the rest of my gender, but I'd just as soon not cripple myself."

"Yet you go barefoot every chance you get."

She shrugged and smiled. "Habit. Left over from my youth when my mother swears I ran around half the time like a hooligan."

"I can't imagine Vi calling you a hooligan." His hand slid farther down on her hip.

"Oh, I've been that and more. In the very best way, you understand." She felt his fingers go still against her hip, several inches below her waist.

"What's that?"

"What?" She was stalling. Deliberately. She knew exactly what his fingertips had discovered. It sent a thrill right up her spine.

"Are you wearing panty hose?"

"Well, that's a heck of a personal question to ask a girl in the middle of a dance."

His fingers skimmed the lacy strap he could obviously feel beneath the material of her dress. "Don't tell me you're wearing a garter belt." His voice rasped like sandpaper, sounded almost as though he was in pain.

"Okay, I won't tell you."

His chest rose against hers as he took a deep breath. He put an inch of space between them, although still held her close.

"Do me a favor and don't move for a minute, okay?"

"Against you or away from you?"

"Brat," he said, and shifted his hand up her back, cupped the nape of her neck.

They danced in silence for several minutes. Maybe he was counting the ceiling tiles or crystals in the chandeliers to get his mind and body to settle down, but Jessica couldn't seem to accomplish the same feat. Her desire might not show as blatantly as his, but it was fairly howling through her veins.

"Thanks for coming with me tonight," he said softly.

"Thanks for inviting me. I've had fun."

The music ended and he took her hand and led her off the dance floor, retrieving their shoes as he went. "Ready to duck out of here?" he asked.

"Can we?" *Should we?*

"Sure. We can do anything we want."

That wasn't exactly true. Circumstances of birth and a business partnership they'd had no say in prevented them from acting on the desire that constantly simmered between them.

Her feelings for Nick were changing faster than she could keep up with. He kept surprising her, showing her another layer of himself, making it increasingly harder to resist him.

THE RIDE HOME was done in silence. Jessica wasn't sure what to say, where to put her hands, how to act. Her mind was consumed with Nick, his scent, his presence beside her, the remembered feel of his body against hers as he'd held her in the dance, discovered the garter belt beneath the fabric of her dress.

When they pulled up in front of the house, she was reluctant for the evening to end. Tonight felt somewhat like a fairy tale. Where anything was possible.

Stars twinkled in the vast night sky. The quiet of the country was accompanied by the high-pitched song of the insects.

Jessica's insides trembled. Since this wasn't officially a date, she shouldn't expect a good-night kiss. Except her desire was stirred to the point where she wanted much more than a kiss.

He opened the front door and she quickly stepped past him. She wasn't tired, but she felt awkward.

When she spied Nick's guitar case leaning against the back of the couch, she went over and picked it up. With the lamps on low, she could see past the wall of windows and doors to the pool beyond and the magnificence of the landscape.

Opening the case, she started to lift the guitar out, then glanced at Nick. "May I?"

He shrugged, shoved his hands in his pockets, then leaned against the end of the wall unit that held the television and a sophisticated stereo system.

She took out the instrument and ran her hands over the smooth wood. "Would you play something for me?"

"Wouldn't you rather I put on a tape or CD?"

She shook her head. She wanted to watch his hands on the strings, the concentration on his face when he listened to the music, chose the chords.

"I don't usually do private performances."

"Then pretend there's a huge audience in the room." She rearranged the decorative pillows on the couch. "There. These are people."

He grinned, took the guitar from her. "I don't have that great of an imagination."

"Sure you do." She made herself comfortable on the edge of an overstuffed ottoman as Nick lowered himself to sit on the coffee table in front of her.

He took a pick out of the decorative glass dish beside him and strummed a few chords.

"What do you want me to play?"

"Surprise me."

He glanced at her, then gave his attention to the guitar. For a few minutes he simply stroked what seemed to be random chords. Then the notes began to take on life. Slow and sultry.

It took her a moment to recognize the tune.

He began to hum and then to sing. The tune was "Lady in Red."

Chills raced up her arms. His baritone voice was more than good. He should have been center stage the other night at the club, not in the background.

He looked at her as he sang part of the lyrics and hummed the rest. It was clear that he was singing to her, about her…serenading her.

Emotions overcame her, swiftly, powerfully. She didn't know whether she wanted to weep or laugh with joy.

He kept his gaze on her as he continued to play. She leaned forward, felt as if the room swayed. The pull of attraction was so strong the air seemed to vibrate. When he flattened his hand over the strings to stop their sound, she gave a start.

Carefully he laid the guitar aside. The silence in the room was nearly deafening. Then the grandfather clock in the hall chimed twelve times.

It was time for Cinderella to leave the ball.

She might have had to strength to follow through on the impulse, but Nick dropped to his knees in front of her, placed his hands on her thighs, inching his fingers toward the hem of her dress, stopping short of slipping beneath.

She hardly dared to breathe.

"Tell me this isn't a good idea," he whispered.

"This isn't a good idea." There were no teeth behind the words. Simply an echo of need, an underlying invitation to go with his instincts, put out the fire simmering inside her.

His fingertips slid farther up her thighs, until they reached the top of her stockings. "I wish you hadn't told me what was under here."

"I—I don't think I did." Her breath was coming faster now. "I think you stumbled on that on your own."

"Did you dress with me in mind?" he asked softly.

Did she? "Maybe," she admitted.

He gazed into her eyes. "I did you wrong the other night. I owe you better."

She frowned, not understanding. Then he stood and lifted her in his arms.

"Nick?"

"You deserved to be wooed, to be celebrated, to have a man take his time, worship every part of you. That's what you missed on the sofa at the office. That's my fault. And I intend to make it up to you."

She might have taken exception to his bold statement. He had a bad habit of informing rather than asking.

But at that moment, he lowered his head and pressed his lips to hers. Tenderly. Sensually. Expertly.

"Let me make it up to you," he whispered. "Please say yes."

Any objections vanished like clouds in a brisk wind. She wrapped her arms around his neck, trusted him not to let her fall. "Yes."

Chapter Twelve

Nick carried her up the stairs and into his bedroom. He'd never carried a woman to bed before, but somehow, Jessica inspired that romantic notion.

He intended to keep his word, show her what making love could truly be like. She'd trusted him to be her first lover, and he'd mishandled that trust. Not deliberately, but that didn't matter.

She'd more or less given him the go-ahead the other day, telling him she was adult enough to have a relationship, that she hadn't asked for or didn't want a commitment from him.

Normally that would be music to a man's ears. In this case, it was like a dare. He wanted to show her that he wasn't so forgettable. That he wasn't stuffy. That he could be tender and giving.

That she should never settle for someone who wouldn't cater to her needs, her pleasure.

Even if that someone couldn't be him.

He forced the thought from his mind, concentrated on now. This moment. This woman.

His heart thudded against his chest as he lowered her to her feet beside his king-size bed. For a long moment he simply looked at her, absorbed every inch of her with his gaze, imprinted the image on his mind.

The red dress caressed her body like a lover's hand—softly, snugly, teasingly. Spaghetti straps left her shoulders bare. The sweetheart bodice followed the swell of her breasts, making his breath catch. The hem stopped a couple of inches above her knees.

And beneath that hem was the mystery that had been tantalizing him ever since his fingers had made a discovery on the dance floor.

"Maybe we should lower the lights," she said, licking her lips, her gaze skittering away from his.

He didn't want to make her uncomfortable, but he shook his head. "I intend to unwrap you. Slowly. Like a gift—the kind where I think I know what's inside, but I'm not sure. With the anticipation of surprise."

"What if you don't like the surprise?"

"Oh, I'll like it." He unzipped the back of her dress, pressed his lips to the curve of her neck, her jaw, rubbed at the gooseflesh on her arms, then slowly slipped the straps off her shoulders.

The silk clung to her breasts, then whispered to her waist. "You are so perfect."

He cupped her breasts, feeling their weight, worshiping them. The skin was so soft, giving, as he stroked and squeezed.

"Nick..."

He kissed her lips, stopping whatever she was about

to say, whether it be protest or encouragement. With his fingertips, he skimmed the dress over her hips and let it drop at her feet.

He wondered if a man of thirty-three could have a heart attack. His heart was racing like a piston, knocking against his chest so hard it was almost painful.

"I knew it," he whispered, surprised he could even speak. Her garter belt was flesh toned, a combination of smooth satin and delicate lace. Straps hooked to the tops of her nylons, leaving her upper thighs bare. She wore firecracker-red bikini underwear beneath the sexy garter, making his fingers itch to peel it away to reveal the secrets beneath.

He cautioned himself to go slowly. He wasn't through unwrapping.

He lowered her to sit on the side of the mattress, then knelt between her thighs, taking his time as he unhooked first one stocking strap and then the other. Slowly, erotically, he rolled the silk nylon down her leg, caressing, massaging, letting his lips follow the path his fingers took all the way to her toes.

He heard her swift intake of breath, felt his blood pump hotter.

He treated the second leg to the same ministrations, then kissed his way back up her calf to her thigh, spread her legs and kissed her through the siren red fabric of her panties.

Her hips bucked. "I'm not sure..." Her breath caught again as he slid the material aside, used his tongue to arouse, to silence her objections. She tensed, indicating this was a new experience for her.

Good. Another first.

This first, though, would be done right. She would remember it for a long time.

He urged her to lie back on the bed, kissed and caressed her breasts, her stomach, her fingertips as she tried to reach for him.

Then he slid her panties over her hips, down her legs. ''Close your eyes,'' he whispered.

Jessica whimpered. She didn't know if she *could* close her eyes. She felt out of control, needed to find an anchor in the storm that raged through her body.

She felt his warm breath, the rasp of his tongue and slammed her eyes shut just as a kaleidoscope of colors burst behind her lids. She gripped the satin bedspread, gave a thought to the possibility of ruining it.

But thoughts flitted away as fast as they came. Everything around her narrowed to an erotic cocoon of sensation. Exquisite sensation.

Emotions built inside her, screaming through her blood, pounding in every pulse point. She couldn't hear for the roaring in her ears. Pleasure engulfed her, filled her from head to toe, stunning her.

Her world teetered on the edge of madness. Sanity came only in snatches of thought. And still he took her higher toward the peak, over and over again. She should call for time-out, but the words wouldn't form.

Then his hands cupped her behind, lifted her, and

with one more clever sweep of his lips and tongue, she came apart, gasped for air, for respite…for more.

She was dizzy from the pleasure, but greedy. She levered herself up, caught him off guard, tore at his shirt and pants.

"I want to feel you. All of you. Hurry." Her nerve endings were still humming, throbbing. Every part of her skin felt sensitized.

Once his clothes were off, she tugged him down on top of her, pressed against him, torturing them both. He could so easily slip inside her body, yet he didn't.

Frustration mounted. She kissed his neck, nipped at his shoulder, then reached between them and took him in her hand.

"No…Jess."

"Yes, Nick." She saw sweat drip from his hairline, saw his jaw clench in an effort to stay in control.

She wanted to shake that control.

Drawing up her knees, she guided him exactly where she wanted him and lifted her hips, urging him, reveling in the hot sensation as at last he filled her.

For endless moments he didn't move, simply pressed high and hard into her as though determined to make them one. Her body throbbed around him, pulsing, squeezing, as something incredibly wonderful built deep inside her.

Suddenly he pulled out of her, yanked open the nightstand drawer and ended up dumping the contents on the floor. For a minute she was confused, didn't understand why he'd stopped.

"I forgot this before. I'm not taking any more chances." In between kisses, he managed to get the condom package open and the protection rolled onto his erection.

Taking advantage of their positions, she shoved at his shoulders, keeping him on his back, then rose to straddle him.

"No. I told you this time's for..." His words ended on an oath and a swift breath when she lowered herself onto him, moved against him, over him, around him.

"This time's for us," she finished for him, and marveled at the different sensations that were once again building. His chest was wide, his hands strong where they gripped her waist, encouraged her to keep moving.

Pleasure spiraled, and then so did the room when he rolled her over, loomed on top of her, kissed her lips with a tenderness that was in direct contrast to the slam of his body against hers.

She cried out. It was so good. So different. So perfect. She rode the crest of another climax, begged him to join her. He took her to heights she didn't know existed, eased her down, then took her back up again. She was nearly sobbing when at last he called her name and buried himself deep inside her, once, twice more, then went still.

Jessica could hardly breathe. She felt as if she'd run a ten-mile race in one-hundred-degree weather. Her body was spent, her limbs numb yet humming, if that was possible.

She stroked her hand over the slick skin of his back.

"Who won?"

He chuckled and shifted off her, bringing her against his side. "By the sound of that little scream of surrender, I think I did."

She tweaked his chest. "I think I recall someone else in this bed losing control. Want to rethink that decision?"

"Why don't we just call it a draw?"

"I like that. We're even."

He stroked her arm and kissed the top of her head. The word *even* made her think of business for some reason. That was an area where she still didn't feel they were equals. But she desperately wanted to remedy that.

She propped herself up on an elbow and pulled a pillow between them to cover her breasts. She still wasn't totally comfortable with her body so blatantly uncovered.

"I've been working on an idea that I think you'll like."

"Does it involve sex? Because I've got to tell you, Red, I'm pretty well spent."

She laughed and pecked a kiss to the dimple in his cheek. "It could involve sex, I suppose. But that's farther on down the line. What I'd like to propose is building a resort hotel in Bridle, close to the Desert Rose Ranch."

He frowned, turned his head against the pillow to look at her. "That town's too small to support a hotel,

Jess. Besides, Coleman-Grayson is into investing, not building."

"There's nothing wrong with change, branching out and becoming more diversified. My father, your father and even you have all played a different part in taking the company in new directions, growing it." She was making a mess out of this, leading with her emotions.

"Wait right here." Grabbing his shirt off the floor where he'd tossed it, she threaded her arms through the sleeves and raced to her room for her project folder.

By the time she got back to his bedroom, he was sitting up in bed, his back against the headboard, the sheet covering him to his waist.

Climbing into the middle of the bed beside him, she said, "Look, I've pulled all the information on the area, the population, potential growth, proximity to airports, freeways and tourist attractions. I've got an estimated-cost report. Everything."

"I don't know...."

It annoyed her that he didn't immediately embrace her idea. Never mind that it was good business practice to study all the angles, to be cautious. He didn't even bother to open the folder. She was proud of her attention to detail, her thoroughness.

Okay, so maybe sitting in bed after fabulous sex wasn't the best place to pore over reports. But she could still state her case, give him a visual.

"It makes perfect sense, Nick. I'd propose we go in under our own flag—Coleman-Grayson. Our name and reputation are legendary in the breeding and horse-racing industry. We'd be recognizable, wouldn't need to rely on one of the other big hotel chains to get us off the ground. We'd be starting from the get-go with our own built-in clientele.''

''How do you figure that?''

''Do you realize how many high-class wealthy visitors and clients the Desert Rose ranch has from out of the country who come to inspect, buy, breed or train their horses? Jabar, our foundation stallion, came all the way from Sorajhee. Aunt Rose brought him when she brought the boys more than twenty-five years ago. The bloodlines are impeccable and known worldwide.''

Even though she knew Nick was familiar with the practices and history of the Desert Rose, she felt it needed to be reiterated. After all, *she* had lived there. She'd seen firsthand. He hadn't.

''People who invest in horses have money to spend, Nick, and they expect comfort, are used to opulent surroundings. For heaven's sake, some of them travel with entourages.''

Despite his silence, which she read as skepticism, she was excited by her idea. She just knew it could work, given a proper chance. ''Coleman-Grayson has the resources to provide that. And we wouldn't have to stop at Bridle. We can seek out sites around other large horse ranches...and race tracks, even.''

''Whoa—''

She put her fingers over his lips. She didn't want an argument to spoil what they'd just experienced together in this bed.

"I know, I know," she said. "One thing at a time. It's just that I have such a huge vision. The potential is unlimited."

"It's a lot to consider, Jess."

"And that's all I'm asking—for now. To consider it. Look, the Fourth of July holiday is this Thursday. My folks are expecting me to come to the ranch for the annual celebration. Why don't you come with me? We'll take a few extra days and scope out the area. Let me show you the site, the figures I've put together."

She nearly said, *and get my dad's opinion,* but didn't want to make him feel as though she was undermining him or discounting him.

Especially since by rights she had more voting stock than he did. He'd never actually said that point bothered him, but if their positions were reversed, she might feel vulnerable.

She didn't want either of them to feel vulnerable. She wanted them to be equals.

And this project could well accomplish that, put them both on the same upward ladder at Coleman-Grayson.

She pushed her hair out of her face and tucked it behind her ear. "Please?"

He nodded, stroked his knuckle gently over her cheek. "You're a hard lady to resist."

Oh, the intensity in his eyes set her blood singing. There was reserve and surrender, and something more she couldn't identify, but right now she didn't want to analyze him. She only wanted to love him.

Oh, my God. Love. She swallowed hard, tested the word in her mind again. In her heart.

Yes, it fit. It had fit since she was a girl.

But now was not the time to admit that particular vulnerability. She didn't want to scare him off as she had years ago.

Right now was the time to explore more of that heady desire that winged through her stomach, the desire she could see echoed in his eyes as his gaze caressed her skin, the deep V opening of the shirt, her bare thighs.

Slowly she unbuttoned the shirt, lowered her body to his and positioned herself on top of him.

"Then don't resist."

THE FOLLOWING THURSDAY, Jessica talked him into taking the Corvette to Bridle—with the top down, of course.

Her first choice had been the Harley, but they wouldn't have been able to carry their suitcases. And with her laptop computer and all the reports she'd put together on the proposed resort, she couldn't begin to fit everything into a backpack.

It was a glorious day for the four-hour drive from Dallas to Bridle. The smell of fireworks wafted on the breeze. Overanxious kids couldn't wait until evening to light their firecrackers and set off their bottle rockets.

The celebration picnic at the Desert Rose wasn't until Saturday, but Jessica and Nick had decided to travel on the day of the holiday, make it a long weekend interspersed with a little business.

"Did you talk to your parents?" she asked over the howl of the wind, adjusting her sunglasses so the stray hair that escaped her braid wouldn't slap her in the eyes.

"Yeah," Nick said. "They're going to drive over on Saturday—or they might take the company plane. They haven't decided. Chase flew off the other day to do an endorsement ad for one of the race-car sponsors. Mom and Dad wanted to wait for him to get back so he could go with them."

"That's understandable. They see him so seldom these days."

Nick glanced over at her, his sunglasses shading his eyes. "Chase *does* do a lot of traveling."

"Yes. Isn't it exciting?"

He turned his gaze back to the road, but Jessica got the feeling something had displeased him. He wore a white polo shirt tucked into a pair of well-worn jeans. His tanned forearms flexed as he gripped the steering wheel.

"You have a yen to travel?" he asked.

"Sure, doesn't everyone?"

"No. Not everyone. Some of us stuffier types are content to set down roots and stay put."

She wondered why he was bringing up the stuffy business. She'd apologized for typecasting him. He'd certainly proved her wrong in her assessment. Heck, he'd even tossed his guitar into the back seat of the car, said he might be amenable to entertaining before the fireworks show at the ranch.

She recalled, though, that when Nick got together with family or friends, he was quick to laugh, fun to be around. He'd just been holding that part of himself in reserve when it came to her.

But that was changing.

So many things were changing.

Before they reached Austin, they turned off the interstate and headed west toward Bridle. The area was lush with trees, the landscape surprisingly green for this time of year. The hot Texas sun took its toll on nature, but the area had seen a good amount of rain recently.

The closer they got to the Desert Rose, the more Jessica's stomach fluttered. She'd spent her life on that ranch. It was home. Her family was there, her memories.

Even some of her fondest and most heartbreaking memories of Nick.

The small town of Bridle was just off the main highway, but they bypassed the turnoff and kept going in the direction of the ranch.

"You look excited," Nick commented, taking his eyes off the two-lane road to glance at her.

"I've missed being home."

"Weren't you the one just a while ago telling me you had a yen to travel?"

"Of course I'd love to travel—just as I've enjoyed it in the past. But that doesn't mean I don't miss being home." She frowned at him, something she couldn't quite put her finger on bothering her. "What are you getting at, anyway?"

He sighed. "Nothing. Can't I strike up a conversation without you getting testy?"

"Normally that wouldn't be a problem. It's your tone, I think. It's as though you're goading me into admitting something. What it is, I have no idea, but it's bugging me."

"Fine. Forget I said anything."

She crossed her arms and looked out at the mesquite- and oak-covered hills. *Fine.* Why in the world did he make her feel as though she was irresponsible because she liked to travel? There'd been an underlying smirk...yes, darn it, she'd heard a smirk beneath his words, a dare—disapproval.

Hadn't she? Or was she so desperate to hold on, for everything to be perfect, that she was reading in dissension where there was none?

She started to apologize, then decided against it when she looked over at him. He was in a snit. She could tell by the way his jaw flexed, by the way his large hands gripped the steering wheel.

If he was upset, it must have been because she'd touched a nerve. And if she'd touched a nerve, then he *had* been baiting her for some unknown reason.

Criminy. The day was too gorgeous to piddle it away being annoyed.

She inhaled the familiar scent of grazing land and ranch animals, knew they were getting close to the Desert Rose.

The last thing she wanted to do was arrive under a black cloud. When she'd left home last, she'd been squawking about having to deal with Nick Grayson. It wasn't going to make a good impression if she arrived with him and they were still at odds.

She gave him a playful punch on the shoulder.

His head whipped around. She couldn't tell if he was glaring or not, not with his sunglasses. But the familiar lines creased his forehead, indicating a frown.

"Lighten up, Grayson."

"Seems like you ought to take your own advice."

She laughed, the sound snatched away in the breeze. "You're absolutely right. I've lectured myself on the very subject," she teased, "and have vowed to heed my highly intelligent, though silent, advice. I can assure you, I'm light as a feather."

His lips twitched. "I have no idea what you're talking about."

She grinned and stuck out her hand. "Are we pals again?"

He looked at her for a long moment, then took his right hand off the steering wheel and gripped hers. Electricity shot up her arm. What she'd intended to be a lighthearted ice breaker became something more.

They could agree to be pals, but their relationship had already progressed way beyond that. They couldn't turn back the clock. But there was every possibility that one of them would have to walk away.

She glanced up in time to see them heading toward a curve in the road and a very large tree. "Watch out!"

He snatched his hand back and swore, righting the car.

"Damn it, that's the problem. I'm too distracted by you."

"Oh, that's right. Make it my fault."

"I'm not making it your fault. I didn't say *you* distracted me. I said *I'm* distracted *by* you."

Confused, she gaped at him. "Have I just been insulted?"

"No, you damned well have been complimented."

It took her a minute to piece it together. Okay, he was blaming himself, taking responsibility. She was a distraction for him.

She felt a smile grow from deep inside her. Well, imagine that. Perhaps there was hope. Perhaps she could distract him from throwing up a shield with regard to a relationship between them.

We'll just see how well your attention span holds, she thought, and turned her head so he wouldn't see her grin.

Chapter Thirteen

"There it is," she murmured when Nick turned off onto the private road leading to the Desert Rose. The sprawling hacienda-style, two-story ranch house sat on a hill overlooking one of the many lakes formed by the Colorado River.

As the car churned up dust, they climbed the hill, passing the main barn, which could house up to sixty horses. The barn was connected on one side to an indoor riding ring, and on the other to the outdoor ring, paddocks and pastures. The stallion barn was in back by the bunkhouse.

"Did Mac and Abbie get moved into the guest house?" Nick asked, slowing down to peer through the trees.

There were two guest houses on the property, both of them quite secluded.

"Yes. They're still working on the remodeling, though. Abbie keeps changing her mind and Mac indulges her."

"I guess that's what a man in love does."

She was a little surprised to hear him say those words. They didn't seem in character. Then again, why wouldn't they be? He came from a loving family. He surely wanted the same for himself.

Just not with a business partner.

She didn't want morose thoughts to spoil the happy mood that came with finally being home. "Alex and Hannah and the boys are in the other house."

"I know."

"Did you know that Alex built her an office onto the house so she could set up her own private veterinarian practice?"

"I helped lay the roof, remember? Right before Mac's wedding."

She had forgotten. Probably because they'd deliberately avoided each other that weekend. She'd been busy with Abbie, making last-minute preparations for the wedding. She'd still been making excuses to her parents for why she wanted to stay at the ranch a little longer, put off going to work with Nick in Dallas.

That seemed like a lifetime ago.

"I guess I keep forgetting you're not Chase."

His jaw flexed. "I didn't realize you had that problem."

She laughed. "You took my words the wrong way. I mean, that he's been out of the country and just recently been brought up to speed on all the goings-on. I think that's why he was eager to have your folks wait for him this weekend. He wants to catch up with our family."

Nick went quiet as they pulled up in front of the lovely courtyard that led to the creamy-yellow ranch house, where beautiful stone arches supported a second-story balcony.

He shut off the car and just sat for a moment. "I feel it, too," he said.

"What?"

"The sense of coming home. Our families have always been so close they seem interchangeable. I'd hate to see anything happen to that bond."

"Why are you so sure something will happen to it?"

"History. We learn lessons from our pasts."

"Your brother's past, you mean."

"Lightning can strike twice, you know."

"What is it you're looking for, Nick?"

"Guarantees."

She shook her head, reached for the car-door handle, when the double front entry door swung open, her mother and father coming out to meet them. "That's no way to live your life, Grayson. There aren't any guarantees."

She plastered a smile on her face, hopped out of the car and ran into her mother's arms, hugging her tight, then turning to her father and treating him to the same welcome.

"Let me look at you," Vi said, her blue eyes damp with tears. "You're well? No ill effects from the fire?"

"Mom. That was two weeks ago. I told you I was fine."

"Well, a mother has to see for herself. Nick," Vi

said, holding out her free arm, "it's wonderful to see you, hon."

"Vi." He set down one of the suitcases he'd retrieved from the trunk and kissed her on the cheek. "You're looking as young as ever."

"Oh, you flatterer. I'm still not sure I've forgiven you all for worrying me to death with that surprise fiftieth birthday party."

Vi had been sure her husband, Randy, was falling for another woman when all the while he'd been organizing a surprise—which Nick had been in on. The other woman who'd caused the strife had been a party planner.

Nick shook hands with Randy, then lifted the suitcases. "Where do you want me to put these?"

"Your usual room. It's all ready for you." It was one of the guest rooms next to Alex, Mac and Cade's old rooms. Vi had always put Nick in the boys' wing of the house.

Jessica had hated it when she'd pined so for him as a girl on the bud of womanhood. Then she'd been thankful for it after that horribly embarrassing kissing experience.

From then on, they'd been civil enemies in public and rarely saw each other in private—thus never having to test their actual civility to each other.

My, how things had changed. Oh, they still fussed over little things. And he annoyed her more than anyone in her life ever had.

But it was a different kind of annoyance. A different kind of fussing.

Now there was intimacy.

And they both, in their own way, were fighting that intimacy like mad.

"You can drop my bag off in my room," Jessica teased, and nearly laughed when his brows shot up. She grinned. "You do remember where it is, don't you?"

"I don't think I've ever been to your bedroom," he said a bit uncomfortably.

She could tell he was trying his best not to glance at her parents. She ought to give him a break, but some devil in her urged her on.

Guarantees, indeed. Someone needed to shake up this man.

"Well, then, follow me and I'll give you the private guided tour. Just let me grab your guitar first."

She dashed back to the car, plucked the case from the back seat and trotted back to him. "Ready?"

Vi and Randy didn't appear to see anything amiss, were already moving into the foyer. Nick, however, was glaring at her as soon as they turned their backs.

"What's the matter with you?" he hissed. "Nothing like inviting me to your bedroom right in front of your parents."

"Well, where in the world is your mind, Grayson? I only asked you to deliver my suitcases, not sleep with me."

"Damn it," he whispered. "Would you hush?"

She grinned and took her suitcase from his hand

once they got inside, passing him the guitar, instead. "It'll be your fault if you need me and can't find me," she said softly.

Then she raised her voice. "I'll run my bags up to my room and save Nick from taking the long way around to his room." The boys' wing was easiest to get to through the back stairs off the kitchen. "I'll be back in a flash. In the meantime, don't let Nick hide that guitar. He's promised to be the entertainment Saturday night."

"Oh, how lovely!" Vi exclaimed. "When did you take up guitar, Nick?"

Nick glanced at Jessica. "Thanks a lot, Red."

"Any time."

JESSICA SHOULD have known that her family wouldn't wait until Saturday's celebration to visit. That night, though she and Nick were tired from traveling, company arrived in shifts—just to say hello and give a hug, they promised.

The quick visit turned into wonderful chaos, with crying infants, laughter and everyone talking over one another.

Jessica was in baby heaven and didn't know which little one to get her hands on first. Alex and Hannah's twin boys were four months old now, both resting in their infant seats, sleeping like lambs through all the noise.

Cade and Serena's twins, Zachary and Natalie, were two months old, and were responsible for the crying jag—one had started fussing and disturbed the other. Serena began to nurse one of the babies while Cade soothed the other.

Mac and Abbie's little girl, ten-month-old Sarah, was crawling everywhere, pulling herself up with the aid of the coffee table and bouncing on her chubby legs, putting on a show.

Jessica scooped up Sarah and showered the baby's sweet neck with kisses, rewarded by the heart-stirring sound of high-pitched giggles.

"You get her wound up, Husky, and you get to keep her over night," Mac said.

"Mac, don't tease," Abbie admonished her husband.

"Husky?" Nick asked, sitting down on the couch beside her.

"Oh, he thinks he's so cute," Jessica explained, taking a moment to give a mock glare at Mac. "He likes to tease me about having two different-color eyes—like a husky."

Nick gave a low whistle. "And you let him get away with that?"

She set Sarah on the floor and steadied the little girl as she grabbed on to the sofa cushions for support, then plopped onto her diapered bottom. "I like to choose my battles, Grayson."

His brow lifted. "You don't pass up many of them with me."

She grinned at him. "That's because you're special. And you annoy me more than my cousins do."

Several people in the room coughed and uttered oohs.

Vi and Randy appeared to be in their glory, smiling and taking in the Ping-Pong conversation as though all was right with their world.

Looking around, Jessica realized that her cousins were in pairs—and with children to boot. In the past it had been just the four of them—Alex, Cade, Mac and Jessica. Then the boys had married, and Jessica was the only single person in the room.

With Nick sitting next to her, the pair of them gave the appearance that they, too, were a couple.

Did her family notice that there was something different about them? Did it show?

She glanced at her mother, caught her gentle smile. Oh, no. She shook her head slightly, trying to telegraph that Vi shouldn't get her hopes up.

Because surely that was what her mother was doing. Heck, she was probably already sewing bridesmaid dresses.

Off in the distance, a firecracker exploded, echoing in the countryside. All the men looked toward the window, obviously wondering if the horses would get spooked. But there were plenty of handlers watching over the expensive Arabians. More so this particular week because of the season.

"Will that be a problem on Saturday?" Nick asked Alex.

Hannah answered for him. After all, she was the vet. It was her department. "I'm a little worried about a couple of the new mares. But I don't want to sedate them unless it's absolutely necessary. Still, if they spook, I've left orders for someone to come get me, in which case I'll only medicate them enough to take the edge off."

"And since our annual fireworks display will be down by the lake," Alex added, "we should be far enough away from the ranch and the neighboring ranches that it won't startle the horses too much."

"So how's it going in Dallas?" Cade asked Jessica as he paced the floor with one of the babies in his arms. He was the business manager for the Desert Rose Ranch, the one who, other than her father, Randy, dealt the most with Coleman-Grayson and the financial end.

"It's going pretty good." Her gaze darted to Nick. She didn't want to get into a business discussion tonight, hoped Nick wouldn't bring up the matter of the resort before she'd had a chance to fully present her case to him, perhaps even take his input into consideration.

Randy obviously saw the exchanged look and leaned forward. "Are you kids getting along okay?"

"Well, I should hope so. We're living together." She'd blurted the words without thinking, then felt her face burn when her cousins all whipped around to look at her.

"Criminy," she said, backtracking. "Not like that. You all know very well my building was ruined in the fire. I'd have gone to a motel, but Mom insisted I stay at Nick's."

Abbie stepped in to smooth things over. "Well, from what I hear, Nick's got a house big enough to qualify as a small hotel. It was very gallant of you, Nick, to share your space with our Jess."

Abbie had been Jessica's college friend. It had been Jess herself who'd done a little matchmaking and brought Mac and Abbie together. From the look on her friend's face, she hoped Abbie didn't plan on returning the matchmaking favor. What was the matter with everyone all of a sudden?

"Like you said," Nick commented, "it's a big house. And it's worked out for the best, anyway, since Jess made me promise to be at her beck and call twenty-four hours a day, seven days a week."

"Twenty-four-seven?" Mac asked with a frown. Alex, Cade and Randy also appeared highly interested in Nick's answer.

What in the world was he doing? Jessica wondered. Deliberately giving them the wrong impression? Well, lately that couldn't very well be considered the wrong impression, but still. Only she and Nick knew that. He didn't need to air their private business.

Especially since that private business was on such shaky ground to begin with.

Nick smiled, obviously using his charm to fend off the daggers being aimed at him. "She's given me a month to transfer all the business knowledge in my head into hers—knowledge I've gleaned over a ten-year period, I might add."

That garnered him plenty of sympathy. Her cousins

and her father knew how tenacious she could be. Once she decided to do something, she wanted to do it all the way—and at the quickest speed and route.

"That's a pretty tall order to accomplish in a month," Randy said, looking at his daughter with a father's indulgence. He looked back at Nick. "How's it going?"

Here was his chance to tell them about her proposal—before she had a chance to lay it out properly with the facts to back it up.

"She's about the smartest woman I've ever come across," Nick said. "I imagine she'll outdistance us all."

Jessica had been primed to defend her ideas. His compliment deflated the air in her lungs, made her heart squeeze.

Her parents both beamed, and she realized that nobody had bothered to ask what would happen when the month was up.

Nick glanced at her. He seemed to know that she hadn't expected him to compliment her.

Doggone it, he constantly kept her off balance.

And darn it, anyway, why did she have to go and fall in love with him?

When she'd gone to Dallas, she *had* intended to outdistance him. Now she only wanted to be his equal.

But according to him, that was too great a risk. And it wasn't just business, she realized. He was part of the family, as she was part of his. Even if they didn't work together, a rift between the two of them could cause a major upheaval.

The same way Chase's broken engagement had ruined a long-standing friendship.

How did one convince a man who dealt in logic to act on emotions? Take a leap of faith?

She didn't have the answer. And above all else, that was the answer, the information, she needed most.

Because when the month ended, they'd have to make a decision.

Jessica couldn't continue to take each day as it came. She hadn't been totally truthful when she'd told him she didn't want promises.

She did. She wanted a promise of commitment.

THE NEXT MORNING, Jessica joined her parents in the dining room. Nick was already there, finishing his coffee and breakfast.

Ella bustled in. "Sit down, darlin'. I'll bring you in a nice plate of toast and eggs."

"No, Ella. Don't go to the trouble. I slipped down earlier and had a cup of coffee. I'm good for a while now."

"You can't operate on a cup of coffee. You need food. You'll dry up and blow away."

Jessica laughed. "I seriously doubt that. How about if I promise to have seconds of that decadent chocolate cake I saw cooling on the rack by the oven? Will that make up for it?"

"You and your sweet tooth." Ella shook her head and walked away, muttering about kids and nutrition.

"You should eat something, dear," Vi said.

"Mom, you know I'm not keen on breakfast."

Vi sighed. "Yes, I know. I struggled with you for years, certain your brain couldn't function at school if you didn't eat properly."

"Well, I guess my honor-roll certificates shot down that theory, hmm?" She glanced over at Nick. "You ready to take a drive with me?"

"Sure."

"The two of you are going out together? Isn't that wonderful." Randy and Vi seemed very pleased. Thank goodness Nick's parents hadn't arrived yet. Jessica was starting to feel like something was going on between all the parents involved. Like matchmaking.

The problem with matchmaking was the expectation held by the meddling parties. And the pain for the unsuspecting couple if those expectations were made public and the plot—or romance—didn't pan out.

And this plot could crumble very easily. She knew Nick wasn't interested in a permanent union.

Oh, he was attracted to her, that was clear. But he'd made his position clear, as well. He wanted guarantees. And nothing in life came with guarantees.

So unless she could figure out how to change his mind, how to give him those guarantees—aside from her word—she needed to prepare herself for the letdown. Guard her heart against breaking.

It wasn't going to be an easy task.

Jessica kissed her parents, then followed Nick out to the car. Before they could get in, a black limousine pulled into the drive.

"More relatives?" Nick asked when a tall man with a commanding appearance emerged from the car, followed by two women wearing flowing robes and veils.

"That's Sheikh Ashraf Bahram of Munir—we call him Rafe. He's a friend of my cousin Sharif. And that's his sister, Allie, with him and her lady-in-waiting—I believe her name's Leila."

"Lady-in-waiting?"

She shrugged. "It's their custom."

"Do you want to wait and speak to them?"

"Perhaps later." Jessica gave a wave, then opened the car door. "Rafe's probably here to check on buying some more Desert Rose stock. He's quite impressed with our Arabians' bloodlines. In fact, one of our mares, Khalahari, is due to foal soon. Rafe has already purchased the offspring."

"Without seeing it?"

"He doesn't need to see it. The foal was sired by Jabar, and that says it all."

"Jabar? Is that old man still at it? I thought Alex had retired him."

Jessica laughed. "Don't say that too loud. Jabar might hear you." The foundation stud was twenty-nine years old—way past the usual prime. "He's as arrogant as always and he seems to have a thing for Khalahari. None of the other mares can turn his head, but let him get within ten feet of Khalahari and he's ready to go."

"More power to him," Nick said in admiration, then opened the driver's-side door and got in. "So, where to?"

"Downtown Bridle."

"Okay, I can manage that." He started the car and put it in gear.

Jessica saw Rafe pause to glance approvingly at the sporty Corvette. Typical guy. She noticed that Princess Allie was looking at Nick.

Well, who could blame her? Nick Grayson was a hunk. Put him behind the wheel of a white Corvette with a pair of dark-tinted sunglasses and a woman couldn't be blamed if she turned to putty.

Something in Princess Allie's stillness sparked an odd feeling of empathy within Jessica. A woman-to-woman sort of connection—intuition, perhaps. It was as though the regal princess desperately yearned for something. Freedom? Jess wondered. The opportunity to ride in an open convertible and laugh in the wind? The chance to have a man look at her as though she was his world, rescue her from her ivory tower?

Criminy! What an imagination.

The temperature was already climbing, and so was the humidity. The breeze from the open car felt wonderful. This morning, Jessica had neglected to put her hair in a braid, so strands of red curls flew around her face like feathers in a tornado. She gathered the mass in her hand, held it out of her eyes. It was bad enough that the humidity would make a fuzz head out of her. She'd be a sight by the time they stopped.

Nick glanced over at her. "Want me to put up the top?"

"No way." She reached for her purse, rummaged around in it and came up with a rubber band. Tugging her hair into a ponytail, she secured it with the band.

"Now you look like a little girl."

Great, she thought. "Goes to show I'll still be a babe when I'm an old woman."

His grin was so sexy she had to look away. Otherwise she'd be tempted to steer him off in the bushes somewhere and convince him to have his way with her.

Determined to keep her mind on business and off sex, she looked around, bracing as Nick made the turn that led into Bridle.

Surrounded by ranches and farms, the town had three bars, a grocery store, a couple of restaurants and a diner, several boutiques and clothing stores, a library, a town hall that doubled as the sheriff's office, two churches, two schools and one small motel on its outskirts.

It had a quaint charm, which was appealing in itself. And it was only a hop, skip and jump from the bustling city of Austin, where there were plenty of activities for vacationers or clients of the Desert Rose to enjoy.

"That—" she pointed at the nondescript motel as they passed "—is where the sheikh and his people are staying." It was a lucky break, she thought, that Rafe and his royal traveling companions had come to Bridle to check on a horse this particular weekend. It supported her argument for the need for fancier accommodations.

"It doesn't look all that bad," Nick said.

"Of course it doesn't. It's clean and serviceable, although you wouldn't have firsthand knowledge of that, since you always stay at the ranch."

"And I suppose you *do* have firsthand knowledge?"

"As a matter of fact, yes." She grinned. "We had a high-school party here after the prom. The rooms were small, but we were kids and didn't care about that. We just wanted a place to sneak alcohol and stay out late. Problem was, Mr. Bennitt called my dad and a few of the other kids' folks."

"Bet you were surprised to see Randy show up."

"I was more surprised to see the sheriff first. Dad called him and told him to scare us good. Sheriff Ruston even threatened to lock us up in the drunk tank."

Nick laughed. "You probably would have turned that into an adventure."

"Maybe. At the time I was scared silly. Sobered us all right up—although we were doing more pretending to be drunk than actually *being* that way."

"Mmm-hmm."

"Anyway, Mr. Bennitt still owns the motel, but he'd love to retire. His kids have moved away from Bridle and don't want to come back. I think if we made him a fair offer for the property, he'd jump at the deal."

"You're thinking of turning this motel into a resort?"

"Not just this motel. See the property next to it?

There's sixteen acres there.'' She paused. ''I own it. It was a graduation gift from my dad, a piece of property that's been in his family for years.''

''Mmm.''

She couldn't gauge his mood, tell what he was thinking. It was as though a mask had slipped over his face. Maybe she was seeing problems where there were none.

''Come on. Let's get out and walk the lot. I'll show you what I have in mind.''

They spent several hours going over all her reports, walking the acreage, touring the existing motel. He asked questions that she had ready answers for.

But he never gave away his thoughts.

By the time they got back to the car, it was driving her crazy. ''Well? What do you think?''

He shrugged. ''You've got some good ideas. I'd need more time, though, more information in order to give you a solid opinion.''

Opinion? That was it? Jessica simmered. ''I shouldn't have to get your approval or disapproval.''

He glanced at her and frowned. ''My job was to take you under my wing. Teach you.''

Well, he'd taught her plenty. The sexual sizzle between them assured that they were both thinking about that.

Was this what he'd been talking about? Her insides were twisted in annoyance because he didn't immediately embrace her vision, yet at the same time, she wanted to press against him and feel his arousal, the hot chemistry between them.

But did chemistry stay this way after years of being together? What happened when the sizzle settled to a simmer?

Would it be so easy to dismiss anger and disagreements over business then?

She wanted to think so. She *needed* to believe so.

But she could clearly see that Nick was holding back—or pulling back. She wasn't sure which.

Darn it. She'd expected him to tell her she was brilliant, back her up this weekend and help her present the idea to both their families.

After all, most of the major parties would be present in Bridle this weekend—namely their fathers, Randy and Jared, who'd begun this partnership.

Interesting how both sets of parents had been looking at them lately, as though they knew something was up.

Did they worry, as Nick did, about the stability of Jessica and Nick's working relationship?

There was a lot riding on the well-being of this partnership. Especially this potentially new turn in the partnership.

The next generation had stepped up to the plate. Would they be worthy? Would they prosper? Or end up ruining twenty-five years of hard work and friendship?

Chapter Fourteen

Nick was already down by the lake, his guitar case propped against a cypress tree. The men were setting up huge barrels for the barbecue.

The hot sun still shone, but it was the time of day when a light breeze blew and the shadows were long across the landscape. Soon dusk would take over, leading the day into night where bursts of colorful fireworks would compete with the blanket of stars twinkling in the sky.

"Got that charcoal, son?" Jared called.

Nick hefted the bag. "Coming right up." As he went to pour coals in the enormous grills, he spotted Jessica walking toward them. Her attention was focused on her sister-in-law, Abbie. In her arms she carried an infant wrapped in a pink blanket—Natalie, he surmised, one of Cade and Serena's twins. The other babies were all boys.

The sight of Jessica with a baby in her arms caused his insides to turn to mush. She was a natural with kids.

But he had no idea if children and family were in her plans for the near or far future.

When she didn't look up, he turned back to his task, spreading the coals evenly in the bottom of the barrel cooker.

She wasn't actually ignoring him or avoiding him, but ever since their trip into town yesterday, she'd been reserved. Not like someone who hadn't gotten her way, but in a thoughtful, watchful, confused sort of manner.

He didn't blame her. Hell, he could hardly keep up with his own feelings, didn't understand them, couldn't seem to control them or settle on any one in particular. And if *he* was this off balance, Jess was surely in a worse state.

He didn't know why he held back on Jessica's idea. It was a good one. At any other time he would have jumped at the opportunity she'd proposed. She was prepared and thorough. He'd made decisions on less information, less *positive* information.

He had to admit that Jessica was destined to bigger and better things. He'd underestimated her. She was young, ambitious and had fresh ideas.

In the beginning he'd actually worried—expected, even—that she'd get bored with office work, yearning for the outdoors of the ranch. After all, she'd held off coming to Dallas for quite a few months after graduation. He'd thought that was because she was attached to the horse business, not all that interested in the corporate workings of Coleman-Grayson.

Now he knew better. It was because she'd been worried about their ability to work together.

As he had been. Still was.

He wanted some sort of guarantee and knew there could be none. What if his life was too staid for her? He owned a home, had a family and roots in Dallas. She was a free spirit, financially independent, able to take off at a moment's notice—to travel, explore, blaze new trails.

She never hesitated when someone said, "Go." Spontaneity and a lust for life and adventure had her reaching for her purse and saying, "Lead the way."

If he took a chance, asked her to stay with him, would it eventually squash her spirit?

"How's it going, Nick?" Randy asked, slapping him on the back.

Nick set down the bag of charcoal. "Once we get this fire burning hot, it'll be much better. The women are already carrying food out."

Randy laughed. "Vi always tells me it's a guy thing that we get sidetracked. Good thing she has patience."

"And good company," Nick added, noticing that the women were gathered in a clutch, laughing and cooing over the kids. "Makes the waiting easier."

"That it does. So where did you and Jess go off to yesterday? By the time I got home from hauling one of the mares over to Johnson City, it was late and y'all had already turned in."

"It was nice to have an early evening for once—although I enjoyed visiting with your family Thursday night,'' Nick said in case he sounded as if he hadn't appreciated the unexpected company.

Randy laughed and held out an arm, inviting Jared Grayson to come join them. ''I hear you, son. I always thought with all the kids grown, Vi and I would get some peace and quiet. Now we've got grandkids.''

''Stop your braggin','' Jared said, cutting a glance at Nick. It was his and Gloria's fondest wish to have one or both of their sons get with the program, settle down and present them with grandchildren.

''Your day'll come,'' Randy said with a chuckle. ''Mark my words.'' He turned back to Nick. ''You were going to tell me about yesterday?''

Actually, Nick didn't particularly want to. At least not without Jessica's presence. He didn't want to steal her show. But he couldn't be vague. Randy might get the wrong impression.

''We went into town—out by the old motel. Jess is researching the feasibility of Coleman-Grayson building a resort hotel on the property next door, perhaps even acquiring the motel. It's a hell of a proposal, and she's done a thorough job of putting all the projections together. But I'd rather wait and let her tell you the specifics. It'd be her project.''

Randy looked thoughtful. ''Coleman-Grayson's into investing, not building.''

''I know.'' Those had been his own exact words. ''But don't discount the idea until you hear the facts. We've all diversified the company in our own way.

This has the potential to be really big. Bigger than anything the three of us have done to date.''

''Don't tell me y'all are talking business without me,'' Jessica said, coming up beside them. Randy plucked his granddaughter out of her arms, and she instantly felt bereft.

''Nick was telling us you're about to take over the show at Coleman-Grayson,'' Jared said. ''He says you've got a lucrative proposal to put before us.''

She glanced at Nick. He had championed her idea? Darn the man. If he was going to hand out positive strokes, why hadn't he given them to *her?*

The opportunity was ripe to expand on her target goal of building resorts, garner support from her father and perhaps Nick's, as well, push things along a bit. Yet she hesitated.

''I've got some ideas. But I'd rather we all sit down at a conference table sometime soon and fine-tune the facts.'' Nick was looking preoccupied, rather than like a man who'd been talking up her ideas. As if he didn't wholly agree with what he'd endorsed.

Jessica realized this wasn't the right time or place to force his hand. It could be viewed as one-upping him. And she didn't want to do that. She wanted him standing beside her—not behind, before or away from her.

''I'm off the Coleman-Grayson clock for the rest of the weekend,'' she said. ''Come Monday, we'll put our calendars together and see if we can all get our schedules to mesh.''

''There's a girl,'' Jared said. ''Glad to see we finally

have someone on board who knows how to achieve balance.''

Nick raised his brows and Jessica suddenly felt the need to back him up. ''Oh, Nick does a very good job of balancing, as well. And for much more important matters. Dad, did you know that Nick received a service award from Big Brothers of America for his contribution to the community?''

''Hey, that's great,'' Randy said, shifting the baby in his arms to his wife as she walked by. ''And it does my heart good to hear the two of you singing each other's praises.''

Jessica bit her lip, felt a moment of amused frustration. Is this how others had felt when she'd meddled in their lives by playing matchmaker?

She should have noticed the signs before. Both sets of parents were fairly blatant about their feelings. They wanted to see more than a business partnership between their offspring.

And the talk was making Nick incredibly uncomfortable. She could tell by the way he shifted, gazed off into the distance, pretended not to be paying attention to the conversation.

Well, actions speak louder than words, her mom had always said. And his were fairly shouting. He wasn't about to go along with or encourage plans to put them together as a couple.

She felt a piece of her heart break and knew this was exactly what he'd been guarding against from the beginning.

But she'd learned to hide her vulnerability, learned to be an excellent actress. She'd make it through the rest of the weekend, she told herself. Guard her heart and her words.

And on Monday, not only would they have a meeting of schedules, she and Nick would make a decision. Once and for all. They were either going to have a personal relationship or make a clean break.

She couldn't wait a month. She was in too deep. She needed to get out while she could. If that was what it came to.

"Speaking of praises," Jessica said, "Aunt Rose and Zak just got here."

Jessica admired her aunt. Rose had been a real-life queen, had married the love of her life. She'd borne three sons and had another one taken from her at birth. She'd been locked away in a sanatorium, yet she'd never lost her spirit or her love for life or her family. Now she'd found romantic love for the second time and was still the queen she'd always been destined to be. And she'd found her way home.

It was a fairy tale come true. And that was what Jessica wanted.

Her own fairy tale.

Judging by Nick's withdrawal over the past couple of days, it didn't look as if that was in the cards.

But they still had the weekend. And she could hope.

"The meat's in the cooler over there. Don't y'all burn those steaks now," Jessica said. She turned as though she didn't have a care in the world and headed over to greet her aunt.

NICK COULD BARELY concentrate on the chords he was playing. He kept messing up. This was probably why his family never pressed him about his Wednesday-night gigs. They figured he was just so-so on the guitar and didn't want to show up and embarrass him.

Well, damn it, he knew how to play the guitar. But what he couldn't stand was sitting here watching Jessica laugh and clown around and dance with his brother. Chase was the kind of guy who drew women. He had a love of life and an easy way that made women fall for him.

And it was none of his damned business who the hell she danced with.

When he hit the next sour chord, he grinned and set the guitar aside. "Must be the humidity," he said to Vi. "Fingers keep slipping off the strings."

She patted his thigh. "You go on and enjoy the night. No sense in you being stuck here trying to entertain."

Trying and failing, he added silently. What the hell was wrong with him tonight? His gut was twisted into a thousand knots. He felt as if his life was falling apart, and he didn't know why.

So many responsibilities rode on his shoulders. He'd always been the one to do the right thing, make the right decision. Chase was the carefree one who pleased only himself.

Nick moved up behind Jessica who was standing now at the shore of the lake, watching as the fireworks burst in the sky and reflected in the dark surface of the water.

''It's beautiful,'' she said, seeming to know that he was behind her.

When he didn't respond, she turned to look at him. Her ready smile froze, faded away.

''I hated it when you danced with Chase,'' he admitted. ''I wanted to deck him for touching you.''

''Nick—''

He shook his head. ''I'm not proud of it, but there it is.''

''Nick.'' She reached out and touched his arm. ''I'm as loyal as they come,'' she said softly. ''If you were to ask me for a commitment, I'd give it to you in a heartbeat. Then you wouldn't have cause to worry.''

''No? What about the next time a man flirts with you? Or if I opposed this resort thing? Would you exercise your voting stock? What wouldn't we fight about, Jess?''

''Love,'' she answered automatically. He was throwing everything at her at once. Grabbing at straws, she imagined. He was pushing her away. And she wanted to cry.

He looked at her as though she'd hit him. As though she'd offered him his favorite dessert, the very dessert he was allergic to and couldn't have.

And in that moment, she knew it was over.

She believed in impulse and love. He believed in

logic and guarantees. There was no easy way to make the two mesh.

"You were right from the beginning, Nick. This isn't going to work. I think you should go now."

He didn't say anything for a long moment. A muscle flexed in his jaw.

Please, she begged silently. *Stay for me. Fight for me.*

Then he nodded, sealing their fate. "What about you?"

She wasn't going to cry. Wasn't going to become the little girl who'd been crushed by her idol. Not again.

"I think I'll stay at the ranch for a few days. I'll rent a car to get back to Dallas or take one of my dad's."

He reached out as though he'd change his mind, take her in his arms. Then his hand fell and he turned and walked away.

Jessica had no idea how she managed to stay upright, how she managed to turn, look up at the sky and watch the next beautiful exploding display. It was several minutes before she realized the blur before her eyes was a wash of tears, which finally spilled over and ran down her cheeks.

NICK WENT INTO the empty ranch house, retrieved his bag and headed back out to his car.

Chase was leaning against the driver's-side door. Nick had seen his brother detach himself from the group of men setting off fireworks. He wasn't in the mood to talk, though.

He tried to reach for the door handle, but his brother was in the way. "Do you mind?"

Chase didn't budge. "You're just going to take off?"

"It's best." He could have physically moved his brother aside. He was a head taller and a good twenty pounds heavier. Instead, he tossed his suitcase into the back, then folded his arms. "It's what Jessica wants."

"Are you sure?"

Nick's nerves were on edge. "Just leave it alone, Chase."

"I'm not a fool and neither are you—at least I didn't think so before tonight. That woman's a great catch."

Yes, and it had bugged the hell out of him to imagine her with Chase—or any other man, for that matter. "Have you forgotten who she is? Have you forgotten the fiasco with Laura? You think it was tough watching Mom and Eve's friendship crumble when your engagement broke up. Imagine what it'd be like with the Colemans."

"You're kidding, right?" Chase shook his head. "There's not one damn thing that's similar between my relationship with Laura and yours with Jess. You and I are two different people."

Nick glared at him.

"Nick, Laura and I were too young. We were in love with the idea of love, and both of us were spoiled. I wanted adventure and she was used to being the center of attention. She was shallow and so was I.''

''Nevertheless, look what it did to Mom and Dad.''

''Did you ever consider that if the friendship between Mom and Eve had been stable, it would have endured? They were acquaintances from college, bro. They hadn't seen each other except for off and on over the years. The Colemans have a completely different relationship. Twenty-five years of history—''

''Exactly.''

''Would you just shut up and listen to me? Hell, you're supposed to be the smart one in the family, but right now you're looking pretty stupid.''

''That's the second time you've insulted me tonight.''

''Yeah, and it probably won't be the last.'' Chase flexed his fist as though he wanted to use it on someone's face—namely Nick's.

''Look, Nick, the Colemans and Graysons have watched each other's families grow up. We've been as close as family. That's a much stronger bond than what Mom and Eve had. Eve was a lot like her daughter. She needed to be the best, needed attention. But she didn't want the wrong kind of attention, and she felt it was a reflection on her if it appeared her daughter had been dumped. She threatened to ruin me, tell anyone who would listen that I'd compromised her daughter, led her into drugs.''

''You?'' Nick couldn't hide his astonishment. Chase might be a hell-raiser, but he'd steered clear of controlled substances, rarely even drank other than the occasional beer. When his pals were drinking liquor, he usually opted for soda.

"Laura had a problem with prescription pain meds. That's another one of the reasons we broke up."

"Why didn't I know about any of this?"

"It was embarrassing. Nerves were raw. I wanted it to just go away. I felt bad for Mom. She was devastated that Eve treated her so badly. And she was worried about me. I asked her to keep the ugliness just between us. I didn't want to drag Laura through the dirt, wanted as few people as possible to know what was really behind the mess."

Chase raked a hand through his blond hair. "The point is," he continued, "there's a bond between the Colemans and Graysons that's unshakable. If their kids get in a conflict, they'll stay out of it. They'd probably feel bad, but it wouldn't shake what they've built. It's family. And if you're too pigheaded to see that, to take a chance…well, you're an idiot." Chase waited a beat to let it sink in that he'd just delivered a third insult.

"Jessica Coleman is one hell of a woman. And if you don't snap her up, then stand back out of my way, because I'd be happy to take a shot."

Before Nick could decide whether to plant his fist in his brother's face for that last comment, Chase turned and walked away.

Nick looked toward the lake. He was too far away to see anyone. Damn it, for the second time in her life, he'd mishandled Jessica's feelings. Hurt her.

And himself in the process.

He got in the car. He had to give her time. Give himself time to process all that Chase had told him. When she got back to Dallas, maybe they'd both have some answers. Right now, though, he wouldn't put her through a scene. She'd asked him to leave, and he would honor her request.

Starting the Corvette's engine was about the hardest thing he'd ever done in his life.

WHEN SHE RETURNED the rental car in Dallas on Tuesday, Jessica called Chase to pick her up.

She sat down on the curb and waited, her insides a jumble of nerves. It had been so difficult to keep a relatively stiff upper lip at the ranch. Now that she was here, there was no family around to keep up the pretense for.

She clutched her handbag in her lap, thought about what was inside. Her father and Nick's had both questioned her request, especially in light of her tears and Nick's sudden departure. But she'd convinced them it was the right thing. The best thing. What she wanted.

The sun was hot, beating down on her jeans, the concrete curb warm beneath her. Dallas was so different from Bridle.

She thought about the ranch, her family, Nick's family. As much as she wanted to make her mark on the world, she wanted home and family more. She wanted love.

She wanted Nick.

But she couldn't *make* him change his belief system. Couldn't *make* him love her, take a chance.

And if she continued to hold on, to hope and dream, what would that get her? Heartbreak.

She'd been waiting for this man since she was a little girl. It was time to give up. She'd tried and failed again. To continue would only cause both of them misery.

Chase pulled up in his father's Suburban.

She climbed into the passenger side. "Thanks for coming."

"You okay, babe? You look like you lost your best friend."

"Maybe I did. Or at least am thinking about cutting him loose."

"My brother?"

"How'd you guess?"

"It's pretty obvious, Jess. He's an idiot. He gets something stuck in his head and he's too stubborn to see what's real. What's in front of his face."

Jessica felt her throat ache with unshed tears. She wasn't going to cry. She was stronger than this. She'd made a decision and she needed to stick by it. For her own sanity. For Nick's.

They drove in silence. When he turned into Nick's driveway and pulled beneath the porte-cochere, he left the engine running. "Are you sure about this?"

"I don't know what else to do."

He glanced over her head, toward the front door, then leaned across the seat and took her in his arms. "You just leave that to me, hmm?"

His hands bracketed her face as he gazed down at her. He looked like a man contemplating some serious kissing.

What in the world? Had she somehow given him the impression that she was interested in—

"Chase?" She was about to ask him if he'd lost his mind when the passenger door was yanked open.

"Nick!" Good heavens. He looked dangerous enough to do some serious damage.

"Hands off, playboy."

Chase smirked at him. Jessica thought that wasn't particularly wise at this moment. Where was the younger man's sense of self-preservation? She hopped out of the truck, hoping to prevent a family clash, and held her breath.

Chase shrugged and grinned. "Better not blow it this time, bro."

"I think I can handle it from here."

Feeling like a bone between the two brothers, Jessica started to simmer. She waited until Chase drove away before she turned on Nick.

His hands were in his pockets. His intense eyes were trained on her. It was as though he wanted desperately to say something, but was holding back.

Jessica's quick temper erupted. This man had made her miserable all weekend, and now she had a thing or two to say to him.

"I don't know what the hell you think you can handle, but let me tell you, buddy, you don't have the batting average that huge ego says you do."

"Jess—"

She talked right over him. "Saturday night, both our parents watched you leave. And they watched me cry. And do you know what they did?"

He shook his head.

"Nothing. Absolutely nothing. They went on with their party. Their love for each other and their friendship didn't even skip a beat. So don't use that cop-out on me anymore. You either care about me or you don't. Quit hiding behind our families'—"

"I care."

"—close relationship. I want more from you, darn it. I want commitment—"

"I love you."

"—and if you can't be man enough to... What did you say?"

His smile was slow and cocky. "You heard me. And if you hadn't shown up here today, I'd have come after you. Chase chewed me out and made me see what a jackass I've been. So, you have to marry me."

She stared at him for a full five seconds. "No."

His expression went from self-assured to stunned. "No?"

"No."

"Why the hell not?"

"Because you didn't ask."

"I just did."

"You did not. You *told.*"

He gaped at her. "Woman, I believe you'd argue with a signpost."

She bit her lip. She'd come here prepared for goodbye, and now she'd been handed her heart's desire.

Nick Grayson loved her, wanted to marry her. Butterflies took wing in her stomach.

"I might. However, I can't have my future husband slipping back to his old ways, now can I? It's been quite a trial training you not to be so bossy."

"Training..." He seemed genuinely at a loss for words.

Jessica smiled. "Nick?"

"What?"

"I love you, too. I've loved you all my life."

Before the words were completely out, he snatched her to him, covered her mouth with his. They stood right there in the front of the house and kissed until she felt dizzy.

"Same here," he finally said, pressing his lips to her temple. "God, I was so afraid I'd blown it, that I'd lost you. You really did spoil me for other women, you know. I couldn't concentrate on anyone else. Every time I'd close my eyes, it was *your* eyes I'd see—one blue, and one green."

He tenderly kissed each of her eyes. "No one had your red hair, your smile. No one was you."

"Oh, Nick..."

"You scared me to death. You looked like a woman, but you were just a girl. It wasn't right, what I felt for you. So I fought it—and then you grew up."

"I can't tell you how happy I am you finally noticed that," she said dryly.

He shook his head, laughed. "Man, I love you, Red. Please marry me."

A smile started deep inside her, grew until it blossomed so wide she thought her face would split. "How about Saturday?"

She watched him pause, calculate, plan. Then he grinned. "How about tomorrow? Or tonight? The pilot can gas up the plane and have us in Vegas by evening."

"Whoa. I love this new spontaneous side of you, but Saturday would probably be better. Our parents will want to gloat over their matchmaking success."

"You have a point." He lowered his head again, kissed her as though she were a fragile piece of china. Jessica had waited a lifetime for this. Just this.

Just this man.

When he finally broke the kiss, she was thoroughly dazed. And so in love she didn't know how to contain the thrilling emotion.

Laughing, he lifted her off her feet and twirled her around. "We'll wait until Saturday, on one condition."

She raised a brow. Now *here* was the bossy man she knew so well. "Already attaching conditions?"

"I think you'll like this condition."

"And that is?"

"Let's start the honeymoon now."

"Absolutely."

Epilogue

Jessica wore her aunt Rose's wedding gown. It was a beautiful creation of satin, lace and pearls, with a train that flowed a good five feet behind her.

She felt as if she was living the fairy tale. At last.

Beneath a gazebo in the lavishly decorated backyard of the Desert Rose, her new husband stood beside her, looking mouthwateringly handsome in a black tuxedo. Chase stood next to him as his best man.

Between the two families and all her new sisters-in-law, the Coleman-Grayson marriage had been planned and pulled off as though they'd had months to prepare.

Jessica took two roses out of her bridal bouquet and went over to her mother and Nick's, kissing each woman and handing her a single flower.

"I love you."

Both Vi and Gloria were crying and could hardly talk.

Jess smiled. "Thanks, all of you, for the push."

"What do you mean?" Vi asked.

"Don't pretend. We know you all were matchmaking."

Her cousins and their wives came up to them. "So how's it feel to get a dose of your own medicine?" Mac asked.

Jessica looked at her cousin, then at her new husband. "It feels wonderful." A thought struck her. She grabbed Nick's hand. "Would you all excuse us for a minute?"

"Hey," Alex said. "You can't start the honeymoon with a yard full of guests."

"The photographer's waiting," Vi added.

"We'll just be a minute, I promise." She pulled Nick toward the house, holding her train so it wouldn't drag in the dirt.

He balked at the back door. "What are you doing? Sweetheart, I'm not stepping foot in that house with you. We'll never come out."

"Come on. I've got something for you."

"Red, there are a hundred people out here watching us. We can't go upstairs together."

She laughed and hoisted up the skirt of her wedding dress. "You know, I never thought I'd say this, but that straitlaced streak of yours turns me on. Wait right here and protect my reputation."

Before he could stop her, she charged up the stairs, her veil nearly flying off. He shook his head. God he loved that woman.

She was back in minutes, carrying an envelope.

Stopping on the back patio, breathing heavy from

her run up and down the stairs, she handed it to him. "I meant to give this to you last Tuesday. But you sidetracked me, and with all the wedding plans, it completely slipped my mind."

"What's this?"

"Open it."

He pulled out the sheet of paper. Coleman-Grayson stock options. His eyes lifted to hers.

"Jess?"

"I talked to both our fathers and they agreed. Both are officially retired." She gazed up at him, suddenly unsure. "I thought it was time we became fifty-fifty partners. For life."

"You were going to give this to me Tuesday? Not knowing whether things would work out between us?"

"Yes. It was my way of giving you my future. It would give you extra leverage if you wanted to oppose my resort project."

He was humbled. "I don't need this to be your partner, Jess."

"I know." She smiled at him. "I guess it's a point in your favor that I forgot the paper and you put this ring on my finger before I gave it to you."

He took her face between his palms tenderly, lowered his head and kissed her. "You are my life, Jessica Coleman-Grayson. I promise to take care with your future. Thank you for trusting me with it."

ALEX, MAC AND CADE held their wives close to their sides, watching as Jessica and Nick kissed on the patio.

"Suppose they'll come up for air long enough to take pictures?" Alex asked.

Cord Brannigan, the young rancher from the Flying Ace spread next door, laughed. "I seem to recall you spent a fair amount of time publicly kissing your bride."

Hannah ducked her head and elbowed her husband in the ribs when he wagged his eyebrows in an attempt to be sexy.

Turning back to their neighbor, she said, "Cord Brannigan, if you're deliberately trying to embarrass me, recall just who it is who tends to the health of your livestock."

He held up his hands in surrender and grinned. "Speaking of livestock, I rescued a heavily veiled damsel on a runaway horse yesterday. She was riding one of your mares, but she wouldn't stick around long enough to tell me her name. I assume you haven't come up missing a horse. I'd hate to think I aided and abetted a horse thief."

Mac laughed. "That was probably one of the sheikh's entourage if she was veiled. They were on the ranch yesterday with Rafe while he was checking on the progress of the foal he's waiting on."

"She didn't tell you her name?" Alex asked.

"Nope. Looked scared to death, though."

"You know," Cade said idly, slipping his arm around his wife's waist, "there used to be a custom in our father's country that if you save someone's life, you become responsible for them."

Cord shuddered. ''No thanks. I'm a confirmed bachelor. I don't know what's going on over here on your ranch with all these weddings, but I can tell you right now it's not going to spill over onto my side of the fence. The only woman I intend to be responsible for is my sister, Brianna.''

While everyone teased and slapped Cord on the back, Nick and Jessica had eyes only for each other.

Their uneasy alliance had blossomed into a love that had the strength to withstand time and squabbles.

And there would probably be plenty of those when Coleman-Grayson began building resorts...or when the children came along...or...

Jessica sighed and placed her hand over her husband's heart. The sizzle between them guaranteed that together they would never have a dull day.

This Desert Rose Bride had finally found her match.

* * * * *